Redwood Lodge
by
Charlotte Picton- Jenkins

Back story!!!

It's not easy living in a children's home. A lot does go one that not everyone may know about, it is completely different to what people might think it is. I want to share it with you all and give you a first- hand experience of what a children's home is all about.

So here I am again writing another book on the same care kid journey. Recently I wrote a book called 'care kid' and people wanted to know more. As before, this is going to be the truth and nothing has been exaggerated or nothings to extreme, it is all true! I have however, changed names for the privacy of the staff that worked there and the other kids that lived there. It's not fair to expose other people by name even if they if they deserve to be exposed. This is my story; everyone has their own story to share.

Care kid is the book I wrote, about me being placed into the care system. I felt like it was important to know the inside truths of the care system because let's face it, it's pretty shit! The best thing about 'care kid' is it's told from a 'care kids' perspective, just like I want this book to be. At the end of care kid, I found my voice and I plan to always be herd. Throughout being in the care system, you tend to lose your identity, instead of being a name all you are is a number, in their very long list.

In the end of 'care kid' I ended up in Woodman's place, I thought that this was going to be my forever after. This is where I was supposed to be until I was 18, this is where I wanted to be until I was 18.

Well, that's what I thought until I was forced to leave Woodman's. They were short staffed, like really short staffed. They had to close for a few months to do a drastic hiring spree, but I knew that I would never be coming back here.

I have been forced to go to Redwood lodge. My mate Brooke used to live there and this was actually the children's home I originally wanted to go to. Although, apparently it wasn't in my best interest at the time. When Brooke lived there, I use to go their all the time- that was until I got banned. How am I supposed to live there, when I am banned?

I did write a journal when I was at Redwood, not about everything, but about most things. I have got a pretty good memory so that helps a lot. I can't promise all of the 'things' are going to be in order because to be honest I can't remember that far back.

This book is going to be different from care kid because in a children's home you have a lot more drama although. These chapters are going to be short stories of what happened whilst I was living at redwood lodge. I can't include everything; otherwise, this would be a very long and expensive book to read. However, I can guarantee I have included all the juiciest bits.

Some will make you laugh, cry and hopefully open your eyes to what a children's home is like. So many people have this mis conception of what a children's home is. I did, when I moved into Woodman's, you only ever know what you are told or what you witness. Social care, Kids homes and care kids is such a big thing and has been a big thing for a very long time, but it is now only started being a topic of conversation.

I will forever miss Woodman's and miss all the people I have met along the way. Woodman's was like another family to me, it was the first time since being in care I felt a sense of belonging. I don't think any other children's home could top this. As you can tell, I loved Woodman's a lot and the people at Woodman's made me a better person. It made me stop doing all of the shit I was doing, it made me grow up and for that I will be forever grateful! Woodman's was my first start, that I so desperately needed.

Elvis; my key worker at Woodman's, the real reason I managed to turn my life around. He helped and guided me, even when I didn't want those things. I was only at Woodman's for 4 months and it's surprising how much one person can affect your life in a short amount of time. I never wanted to disappoint him, he just cared so much about me, that I felt like I just couldn't let him down. He is what a care worker should be and he is a care worker we need more of.

Josie; was probably the person who I was the closest to. We didn't get a long all the time, after all it was an all-girls children's home. Our bond grew when we got to know each other a lot more, she's one of the reasons I enjoyed Woodman's. Miss you Josie, our all-nighters were frankly just fucking funny. Being with Josie felt just like being back at home with Kacey and all the crazy shit we use to get up to.

Evelyn; was the gay of the house and she made that very clear. She is a very funny person and actually I was very close with her, before she ran away.

Even Louisa kicking off and stealing my shit. Like things like that which I fucking hated I am still going to miss because that's what made Woodman's. I am still thankful that I am able to move to another children's home, I mean everyone knows that foster placements just aren't for me.

So, before we get into this story, my name is Immie Taylor, I am 15 years old. Originally from Sudbury, but lived all around Suffolk. I have 1 full sister and 1 half-sister- so yeah, I'm the middle child, such fun. I haven't always been family orientated, but not living with your family makes you realise a lot.

Kacey is the eldest and my full sister. She is my rock, my twin and my best mate. I don't know what I would do with out her. We haven't always been close, but when you don't live with your sister you realise just how much you need them.

Bella, is only little still. So, this is what she knows and I think that is the best out come for her. Of course, she will know when she's old enough, but for now she has a perfect family and life, that is all I could ever want for her.

I have had 3 social workers, been to 5 high schools and had a lot of irrelevant people coming in and out of my life. Here I am starting new AGAIN, for something I couldn't even control. The system chose to put me through this AGAIN!

Even though at Woodman's I manage to sort my life out a little bit, I am still a mess. So, don't judge me because everyone makes mistakes. I am young and I want to live my life how I want to live it; nobody is going to tell me different. I am Immie Taylor and I have a voice that I am no longer afraid to use.

Moving in

This is going to sound weird, but I wanted Elvis to move me to Redwood lodge. Usually, a social worker has moves kids from placement to placement, but I wanted one last key work time with Elvis. He's someone who I truly respect and am so thankful for everything he has done for me. I know I keep saying how much Elvis has done, but he deserves the recognition. There is no amount of gratitude I can give him and he doesn't even realise how amazing he actually is. He deserves a pay rise.

So, I packed up the left-over things in my room and I just looked around the house to make sure I had everything I needed. I mean I didn't want to leave anything here because I don't know how long this place is going to be shut for. Also, to look around the house for the last time was just so sad. To think of how many memories, I have made in this house in such a short period of time is so crazy and I didn't think it was even possible to make lifelong friendships in 4 months.

I had an amazing relationship here with my boyfriend Ryan, had some funny drunk nights with Josie and Evelyn. This was my home so just saying bye to it all, made me cry, don't usually cry in front of people so I was more crying inside and an occasional tear rolling down my cheek.

Just before we loaded things in the car, my door battery died. All the doors at Woodman's were operated by a fob. Which is basically an electronic key. They have an actual key for when this type of things happens, although they couldn't find it.

This was just brilliant, what a way to end my era at Woodman's. This literally just summed up my time here. We had to wait like 30 minutes, I don't even know how hard it could be to find a key for fuck sake. You would think they would store it in a safe place, like with all the other keys they have.

I said 'see you later' to all the staff that was on shift, to me good bye seems permanent and I knew I would see them again. Even if it is in Tesco's or when I'm 18 on a night out. I got in the car, that Elvis put all my stuff in. Just like he took all my stuff out when I moved to Woodman's. I was surprised that all my stuff could fit in because I have way more stuff than I came here with.

Before me and Elvis headed to Stowmarket, we had a little key work time. He took me to KFC to get a Krushem, this was our thing. With key work time we get about £3 to spend on like a drink or a burger or even if we wanted to go play pool or something. Key work time is a specific time to talk and spend time with your key worker, in most circumstances your key worker is someone you feel able to talk to about your life problems with.

Although you don't get to pick your key workers, their like kind of assigned to you as you move into the kids home and you can still ask other staff to take you out on key work time. I was just lucky enough that Elvis was the staff I liked most there.

One of the good things about living in a children's home is there are loads of different staff, with loads of different abilities. So, Elvis is old and he has a lot of life experiences, so he is good at life advice and also listening. Most female staff are better at how to manage your hair and girly advice. So, if you don't feel comfortable to talk to one staff about it, their is going to be some one else you can speak to.

In this key work time Elvis just wanted to know how I felt about the move and what was going through my head. Our conversations just work, sounds like a really weird thing to say, but Elvis is just really good at listening and advice. I usually just rant and rave and he just take it all in and comes up with a good solution. Elvis just gets me!

Then the bit I dreaded; we were on the way to Stowmarket. I called Kacey to tell her I was on my way. She lives at the YMCA, which isn't far from the children's home so she said she was going to come to meet me. Just to make sure I was feeling okay and of course she wanted to see me as well.

Kacey, isn't just my sister, but she's my rock and my best friend. We didn't always get along with each other when we were living at home, but what sisters get along all the time. Since me and her have both gone into the care system, we have noticed how much we truly mean to each other and since then we have always had each other's back. We are in separable, sisters by choice friends by chance.

When I called Kacey, she told me that she would be walking to redwood lodge with, Zak, Azza and Brandon, these all live at the YMCA with her as well. I had briefly met Azza and Brandon before, but I had never met Zak.

I have been going to the YM since I was about 14, so I pretty much knew everyone there, although, just like a children's home, people move in and out all the time. I have already dated 2 guys from there, but let's not get into that.

Zak- I haven't got an opinion yet, but I am sure I will form one very quickly.

Azza and Brandon are basically the same. They both smell and literally don't care about what they look like. All in all, they are just so weird, I know weird can literally mean anything, but that is the only word that best describes them best.

I know when I arrive at Redwood I am going to have to have like a tour and an introduction, but let's be honest I don't need to. I always use to be round here and I know it pretty well. I just want to unload my shit and go out to see Kacey. I don't think at Redwood I am going to be so invested in the house. Like this is the town where my sister lives and we haven't lived in the same town in a long time. So yeah, I am going to be living with the kids here, but I ain't exactly going to be hanging out with them like Woodman's.

We are here in Stowmarket; Kacey and the boys were sitting at the top of the road, they had to wait there, as it was still during school times, but as soon as I was done with everything I was going to meet them up there. So, we drove down the road and knocked on the door. They showed me around and what room I was going to have. The weird thing is I was having Brookes old room, I never saw her room in person, but I use to face time her like pretty much every day.

So, Redwood is laid out differently to Woodman's. As you walk in the side door (the one the kids and staff use all the time as the front door is locked) you come straight into the kitchen, I mean the kitchen isn't that big compared to wood mans, but Woodman's had a kitchen dinner and redwood lodge have a breakfast bar in the kitchen instead. To the left is the lounge which is like a square, so not big, but a lot cosier. Off the lounge was the dining room, it has this big table which just felt more of a family type of vibe. Straight after the kitchen is the hallway, it's a long hall way which goes round the corner and leads to another door and to some more steps, but before you get to that, to your left is the manager's office. To your right is the 'main stairs', then just past the stairs is the games rooms/ study and then the main office. Next to the main office is the 'main' toilet. Which staff use as they aren't supposed to use the one upstairs. Next to the toilet is the laundry room, next to that is the meeting room and opposite the laundry room is a chemical cupboard. I hope you are able to picture this in your mind a little better, it basically is just a home with more extra rooms.

So, as I said at the end of the hall way, you get to another door, go through that door and you come to some stairs. These stairs lead to the flat door, which is semi-independent designed for 16+. Its suppose to help young people when they are thinking of moving into their own flat or into a YMCA . Now because I wasn't going to be going into the flat anytime soon, they said I couldn't look round it, which I thought was kind of bull shit, but who cares. Mackenzie is the only one who lives in the flat at the moment, but Robert should be moving in their soon, as he is already 16, but he just needs to work on his behaviour.

Any way back to the tour- So across from the flat door is another door. To the left of that door is my new room, opposite to that is Robert's room. Next to Robert's room is Mikes room. Then next to that room is Sapphire's room. Just like Woodman's there is a sperate shower room and there is a bathroom. Then you come back to the main stairs. Which leads back to the hall way. And you have done a full circle.

Silver was the one who was giving a tour and she was going into so much detail which isn't necessary. Like I appreciate it and it does make me feel more comfortable about moving in here, but just a waste of time. Sliver is a member of staff, she is polish and has this most amazing accent, really wish I could speak another language. Also, her hair is amazing, it's like green ombre and its silver as well. Goes with the name I suppose!

Everyone helped unload the car and I do really appreciate it. I knew most of the kids here although, we kind of lost contact when Brooke moved, but I hope there is not bad blood between us. The only one I didn't know was Sapphire.

I was sad about rushing off because I still wanted to chill with Elvis a bit more, like I am really going to miss him so much, but when I was about to cry, he dropped the most amazing news. As you know Woodman's is closing down for about 3 months and the staff are being re assigned to different homes around Suffolk and Elvis is coming to work here. I honestly could not be more excited. He is what I need to get through this, he is the light at the end of the tunnel and some normality for me. I don't know why he can't just work here full time and forget about Woodman's.

So, I just said "see ya later to everyone and off I went". I am not a very huggy person, but I gave Elvis a hug. Not sure if your allowed, but he's been a dad to me, so he deserves a hug.

Kacey and that lot was still waiting at the top of the road for me, she even had a fag rolled. Isn't she just so cute! Kacey just knows what I want and need. She didn't roll it, she got one of the boys to roll it, but it's the thought that counts.

Zak use to live at Redwood and he was talking about all the shit he got up to. Like I know living in a kid's home is fun, I was in one before moving here. Like Zak's annoying, he always manages to move the conversation back to him. He is cute, but I definitely go on personalities and I don't know if Zak even has one. The care system is a very small world, feel like everyone knows one another.

I did want to see Kacey and actually hang around people I don't live for a change, but I do also wanna get back and sort my room out because I probably won't be bothered to do it tomorrow. So, I chilled with these lot for a little while, we went to ASDA, which is just down the road from Redwood, Kacey needed to get baccie and I needed her to get me some as well. After ASDA I said "see ya, I will give you a message when I get back." Then I walked back to Redwood.

When I got back, I really wanted dinner and I hoped they saved some for me, I was starving. For dinner they had tuna pasta bake, I don't like fish and I don't eat it because I'm a Pisces. I was fuming! Staff did say they would make me like a jacket potato, which wouldn't be my go-to thing, but I was still thankful for them trying to make an effort and actually give me food.

All the other kids were out on an activity, so I was home alone with Jay (my knew key worker). So one of the great things about living in a kid's home is you have different activities each day. Some of them will be kinda boring, like go for a walk or do some crafts, but most of them are like cinema, roller skating, etc. I think they just don't want us sat in all the time. Some kids are not from the area, so going out and doing activities allow them to get out and do different and exciting things.

Jay; is nice, he is young which means he is down to earth, although that also means he lacks experience. He is the son of Jenny Dean (the manager of all the kids homes). So it is clear how he got this job. Although he is funny and nice to look at.

Now I wouldn't say I have OCD (obsessive compulsive disorder) because I am not clean all the time and I don't spend 7 hours a day cleaning. Although when I do clean, I go a bit over the top, I just like things to have a place and look nice. I like looking after the things I own.

Like when I was putting away things into my room, I literally had to clean all the shelfs and draws first because there was no way I was putting my shit into that without it being cleaned. I wanna know who cleaned this room before I moved in because this just isn't good enough, like it was actually dirty. I didn't manage to put away all my shit because like I said I had to clean it first and that took ages! So hopefully I will have better luck with it tomorrow, but right now I need to sleep, moving is exhausting.

I hope this is the last place I move to before I can actually get my own flat. Yes, I should be use to moving around, but the truth is I'm not. All I have wanted is to find some where I can call home and somewhere I can spend the rest of my childhood. Just have to wait and see if this is the place for me.

Food Fight

Day 2 here and I have settled in really quickly to be honest. Usually, it takes me about a week to get a bit cocky and where I can act my 'normal' self. Whatever that is? I don't know whether being my normal self is such a good thing because then I just don't really care. If I am being honest, I don't think the staff like me any more than they did a year ago, yeah, the kids alright, but this isn't Woodman's.

I was living in Stowmarket and me and Kacey hadn't lived in the same town for like 2 years. Might not sound like a long time, but, me and Kacey are really close and that is a long time for us not to see each other every day. I was going to see my sister as much as possible because even though I wanted to stay here long term I don't think I will to be honest, there was a reason I got banned a year ago.

So, I spent most of the time with Kacey and people that lived at the YMCA. Kacey was closest to Zak, so we kinda just chilled with him mostly. I wasn't 16 yet, which meant I couldn't go into any one's room as it was against their insurance. So, I literally spent most of the time in the kitchen or outside smoking a fag. It was slightly annoying that I wasn't old enough to just chill in Kacey's room, but I will be next year and I honestly just cannot wait for that. Literally going to be spending most of my time here- not like I don't do that already.

Usually with YMCA's you have to be 16 to be allowed on the site because of the insurance like I said. The only reason I was allowed in communal areas was because I was family and that allowed special exceptions. Some staff would allow me to go into Kacey's room, but that was never guaranteed.

In Stow there isn't really a lot to do, I think it's all about the people you know and where to chill. Stow is quiet a small place, compared to most towns any way. I am originally from Sudbury and Sudbury is quite a bit bigger than Stow (I think it is anyways), maybe that's just because I know Sudbury better?

I didn't go back to Redwood until about 9ish, I wasn't sure what my curfew was or even if I had one. I didn't ask, but I am 15 and if I wanna stay out late than I should be able to. It was really cute because Zak walked me back and even gave me his jacket to wear because I was a little bit cold. Kacey didn't walk me back because she is really lazy.

Me and Zak didn't really speak about much, we haven't exactly known each other that long, so I don't really know what we would say to each other. Some of the things he comes out with is literally the biggest bull shit I have ever herd.

Any way when I got back to Redwood staff had like a fat arse go at me because I was home late. I don't understand how they can call this late, when I was 12, I use to be out later than this. Are they serious? For one; they didn't give me a set time when I had to be back, they just said "don't be late." Which is down to an opinion! To me 9pm is not late. If they want me home at a set time then give me a set time to be back, its literally as simple as that. Generally, don't understand what the issue is.

All the kids were in, I didn't know how to act and I wasn't sure what to say, I hadn't spoken to them properly for at least a year and I have never lived with them. This might surprise a lot of people, but I am a shy person. I put on a façade; I act confident when I need to. When it comes to making friends or interacting with kids my own age, I am the shyest person. Everyone has a place and I need to figure out where my place is. There is always a hierarchy where ever you go.

This evening something happened that was completely unexpected and the truth is I am not entirely sure how it happened. I think staff pissed Robert off as he was making a drink and then he lobbed the entire caron of milk across the kitchen, but it accidently splashed sapphire.

So, Sapphire got the entire bottle of juice, opened the bottle and then poured it all over Robert. At this point me and Mike got involved. It ended up being girls v boys. We were getting sauces out of the cupboards, flour, sugar. Literally anything you could think of. It was so funny, but I am not entirely sure if the staff found it funny! Most of the things were in a locked pantry so luckily not all the food was wasted.

Mike was getting fake tan and shaving foam from the bathroom; this was getting out of control way to fast. I'm just not sure how it escalated to this because this was just crazy. There was bbq sauce up over the walls, everywhere stank and so did us kids.

We all cleared it up because we did all feel bad about it, but Robert started this so he should be the one clearing the majority. I just wanna take a shower and wash my hair because I just feel gross. The only person that didn't get involved was Mackenzie and that's because he wasn't here, I think he went out for the night or was staying at his parents, I am not really sure to be honest.

When we were clearing up Kacey face timed me, she was with Zak and a couple of other people, but I am not really sure who? Then Zak just out of know where asked me out, I wasn't expecting it nor did I think he liked me like that. Does he actually like me? Or does he just look at me and think big arse big tits, like most boy do. It was just a bit weird and I didn't really know what to say to be honest so I just said I'm gonna think about it for now.

After it was all cleared up, we all went outside and had a fag. I feel like in most kids' homes, you have to have a night where you kick off and just have a laugh to really get to know the other kids and what their about. It's kind of like a bonding experience.

It's hard for the other kids in the kids home, I am coming into their home and being a part of their little family. It's important that we get along and nowhere the boundaries lie with one another.

I went to bed not long after that because I was shattered, I don't think I was doing much the following day, but I didn't wanna get into a bad routine. I wanna have a laugh, but I still wanna get on with my life. I said Woodman's would be my fresh start, but that got closed down for things out of my control so now I guess it will just have to be Redwood as my fresh start. I am going to have to make the most out of a bad situation.

Halloween

Halloween as a kid meant dressing up and going round to all the houses on your road and collecting sweets. It used to be one of the best times as a kid because who doesn't love free sweets. We always use to go round with our mum and a couple of friends, from our neighbourhood.

Now Halloween is just another reason to get drunk and I ain't complaining about it. I am defiantly not a piss head or an acholic, but yes, I like to get fucked up a couple of times. I am a 15-year-old girl and I don't know many 15-year-olds that don't drink.

Me, Sapphire, Robert and Mackenzie were planning this night for a while, we live in a kid's home it's not like we are made of money so we had to save up for this shit. So originally the plan was we were gonna go out about 7ish, but first Sapphire wanted to pick up, she was more of a smoker than a drinker. Yeah, I have smoke weed in the past, but I am not really about that now because here is supposed to be my fresh start. The way I look at it is, I am probably gonna drink when I am older and have kids and that, but the likely hood of me smoking weed around my kids is none, so I don't wanna touch it.

Before we went out drinking, we met up with Zak and Sam (Sam is someone who also lives at the YMCA). I didn't invite Zak because I just wanted to drink without a guy there. Robert does not count because he's basically a girl and Sapphire was the one who wanted Mackenzie there. There is something going on between them.

Whenever I go out drinking with my boyfriends, they are just too clingy and I am not a clingy type of person. So far, the only boyfriend who hasn't been clingy was Ryan and that is just because he understood me.

Me and Zak are now dating, I will get to that later. I will kinda discuss our relationship and how that happened, but for now let's just hear about a fucked-up night that was truly amazing.

Sam and Zak were only planning to have a few beers in the YMCA anyways so they might as well come out with us. If I am being honest I just kinda felt bad for them, that ain't a way to spend Halloween.

So, we met them and Kacey as she was going to buy our alcohol for the night, we live in a kids home so it wasn't going to be much, but I am a light weight anyways, so I get drunk very quickly and very easily. Which times like this I ain't complaining about. It is always a cheap night out for me. We got a couple of Ciders, Smirnoff ice, vodka and WDK. Me and Sapphire had been saving a couple of weeks for this. Now we had Sam and Zak's money so we had enough to get what we wanted, a little bit for everyone.

The plan now was for me and Sapphire to go back to Redwood to get changed, get a few things to munch on and then head out for the night. Then we were all going to meet at the rec at about 7 as we had already planned. Because Zak and Sam were now coming Mackenzie and Robert didn't want to come. I think Robert knew Zak from Lowestoft and they had some beef or whatever, but I don't exactly know the full story. Robert is just a wet chop and Zak ain't even hard as I said "he's a wanna be bad man". So, he wouldn't do shit to anyone. We tried explaining this, but Robert was scared. We just left it, their loss.

So, at 7 me and Sapphire left Redwood. Sam and Zak met us up the road instead of at the rec because apparently, we were taking forever. We walked down to the rec and it was really annoying because Zak wanted to hold hands all the time. I'm not that affectionate type, not in public anyway. It just cringes me out, like kissing or hugging in public. Not so much hugging, but I think kissing is like a private thing and not everyone needs to see us exchange silva.

I am going to sound so old now, but to me any intimate thing should mean something. I don't think you should kiss someone without any meaning or feeling behind it, it's weird I feel like this considering how I lost my virginity, but the truth is I did lose my virginity to someone who I did love. I think you can love more than one person at the same time. I doubt he felt that way about me, but I don't care. I'm not gonna say how I lost my V in this book, if you wanna know you can go buy my other one!

Down at the rec theirs a picnic bench, I mean there's quite a few, but there's a 'main' one so we all sat on that and started drinking. The recs not huge and I don't know why we didn't sit on the grass like away from where people could see us. To me it just felt a bit bait sitting in the open. Maybe I was just a little paranoid.

Whist we were drinking, we were playing a few drinking games like never had I ever and whoever the bottle lands on has to take a shot. We just wanted to drink as much as the alcohol now because we didn't wanna carry it around with us. I was starting to feel a little bit drunk already, which was a VERY bad thing! I was 15 and I was loving life.

About an hour went past and a car pulled up along the outside of the rec. I recognised the car. Turns out it was the homes car, Tilly and Jay rocked up at our little drinking sesh. I was trying to act sober, but I ain't good at pretending to be sober when I am drunk. At this point I wasn't even drunk, I was gone.

Tilly is another care worker, really nice, classic Essex girl. Very honest and she wasn't afraid to be honest neither. She was refreshing to be around.

Jay said "are you guys coming home?" I don't even know why they are following us around and wanting us to come home now. Do they really think we are gonna come home now? I'm drunk, I'm not going to listen especially if it's something I don't want to do! They just need to chill and know even if I am drunk that I can look after myself and if that fails, I have people that can look after me instead. It's not like I am drinking by myself, it's called a night out for a reason. Yes, I am underage, but I could be doing worse things than getting drunk in a park. Like its good I'm not doing heroin on a public toilet.

We were going to go back to Redwood because we were hungry and wanted something to munch. We just didn't want to let Jay or Tilly know that because then they would ask a lot more questions. If we just ignore them then hopefully, they will just go away.

Redwood isn't far away from the rec so the walk wasn't that far, but we met some people along the way, which is why it took longer to get back. I didn't know who they were, but they were mates with Zak, so they were alright with me. Their names were Kiki and Darcy, Sapphire got on really well with Kiki, kinda like they had been mates for ages. I think that took some pressure of me a bit because I was the only one that knew Sapphire, but now she could speak to some one else.

Whilst me and Sapphire went to Redwood, the others waited round the corner, as it was about 9;30 they weren't allowed to come in, Zak was banned anyway and also because we were drunk, I don't think they would of cared about the time. By the time I got to redwood I couldn't even remember why we went there in the first place. So, me and Sapphire tried to get a drink and it was not working out. She was holding the jug whilst I was trying to pour in some juice and it just went everywhere. I think even Jay and Tilly got wet as well, but I am not really sure, it's all just a little fuzzy.

I can't remember the whole thing, but when I think back to that moment, I knew it was funny and it makes me laugh every time. I think most people when they are drunk, are funny any ways. Me and Sapphire are like a duo act, the female version of Ant and Dec. So much love for Sapphire.

From this point on my memory is a little fuzzy even more fuzzy than before and I can remember bits, I just don't understand how it happened or how it got to that point. There is just like a blank bit missing from that night. I remember walking to Kiki's, we were gonna stay there that night. Her mum had no idea that we were planning on staying there, so she's gonna have a surprise in the morning.

Sapphire didn't want to stay as she doesn't like staying round people's houses . Also, Sam was trying to make moves on Sapphire and that just made her feel really uncomfortable. So, I did say if u don't wanna stay you can go, their ain't any issue with that, so we walked her home and then walked back to Kik's

Next thing I can remember was lying on the couch next to Zak, I feel like I was boarder line unconscious. Zak was very touchy as I said he would be, like I'm very drunk and want to sleep. I'm paralytic, can hardly form a sentence together. Can you not touch me right now? I don't think he cared how drunk I was, he just wanted something.

I didn't want to have sex in someone else's house, like that's weird and I have only had sex once, like I didn't want it to hurt again or for me to bleed. And considering me and Zak hadn't had sex before I didn't wanna not remember it in the morning. I like things to have a meaning.

I didn't think he was getting the message clearly enough. Like of course at some point, I wanted something to happen. I just didn't want anything to happen tonight. I don't understand why he wasn't understanding this.

He still continued to touch me and started going under my clothes, as I kept pushing me away it felt like he kept putting more force, I soon just ran out of energy. I couldn't relay to him that I didn't want this, I couldn't speak I didn't have any more energy left to fight. My strength was gone.

That's all I remember; I don't know what else happened. I must of fell asleep, I'm a deep sleeper when I am not drunk so when I am drunk, I'm boarder line dead. I don't know what fully happened. The next day, I wanted to ask Zak, but I didn't want him to think I was being stupid. I didn't feel like we did have sex.

I woke up with all my clothes on, my vagina didn't hurt, but if we didn't have sex what happened? The last thing I remember was him trying to touch me and him succeeding in touching me. I feel sick, I shouldn't have let myself get that drunk to not remember, surely Zak wasn't that drunk to know I was passed out? To accuse my boyfriend of something after a few weeks of being with each other isn't right so I didn't ask. I didn't feel like I could ask.

Looking back, I should of because I would have punched him square in the face and not given it a second thought. I'm a feminist and I believe men shouldn't have their way just because they are men or just because they feel like they can.

Waking up at Kiki's house was so weird. We got a wakeup call by her mum. She was so pissed; she was shouting and yeah, she was very pissed about having strangers in her home. I don't blame her; I would have been exactly the same.

I was pissed that I got woken up at 7:30, by a bitch that was going through menopause, I was confused and very hung over. Like fucking allow me to sleep.

The walk back to mine was quiet, I had nothing to say. Zak and Sam were having a random arse conversation that I couldn't be bothered to listen to or take any part in. I wanted a shower and to eat something. I was dreading what staff was going to say, I knew they had reported me missing.

If you're a kid in care and you don't come back their night, without them knowing, or if your late back for your curfew. Even if you pre warn them you're going to stay out late they still have to report you missing because they don't know what you're doing or who you're with. Being a kid in care your basically not allowed to wipe your arse without them knowing.

I left Zak at the top of the road, gave him a hug and I dodge his kiss good bye. He looked at me funny but I just walked down the road without really acknowledging him. I can't look him in the eye right now. I'm too tired and to confused, just can't be dealing with that.

All the morning staff tried talking to me as I walked through the side entrance, but I didn't acknowledge them. Just got a bowl of cereal and some milk and went straight to my room. Everything was a blur and I kept trying to think back to last night, but even the people began to get fuzzy. I just need to sleep for another 2 hours and think clearly again later.

Love at first sight

Me and Zak met at the YMCA (as I have said). He was good friends with Kacey and that's how we started talking. At first it wasn't anything serious, I wasn't looking to be in a relationship. I was 15 and have already made some pretty bad decisions. I didn't want to make any more any time soon, although by now you know I have already made bad decisions and you already know me and Zak are in a relationship.

This is kinda how me and Zak became an item and what was going through my head, I suppose, before we finally made it official. I didn't know where to put this chapter in because it didn't deserve to go at the front, although that's where it fit best. I think I wanted all of you, to have an inside of our relationship before going into detail. So, from the next line down this is what and how happened.

I really wanted to figure out who I wanted to be, before having to figure out me whilst trying to get to know another person. It's just too much and I don't have the energy for it right now. I haven't always had time to focus on what I wanted, so now was my chance and I had nothing holding me back from doing that.

Zak is like 5ft 7. So, a little taller than me, he's ugly, but in a weird cute kinda way. His teeth are crooked and yellow, he smokes with one lip down and he's got a noticeable moni brow. He's got brown hair and blue eyes, he's chunky and always wears a hat and a hood to cover his hat, with a man bag. I suppose you could say a wanna be road man. Zak always tries to fit in and tries to impress other people. One thing that really bugs me is he always tries and shows off, but with things that just make him sound like a dick.

Let's give you a little back story on Zak; Zak is originally from Great Yarmouth. He used to live at Redwood about 2 years ago. He knows a few people from Redwood, like Robert and Mike, only because they all grew up in the same area. I don't know how Zak ended up moving to Stowmarket, I didn't ask, I am a true believer that people will only tell you what they want you to know, so if I didn't know, he didn't want me to. Also, I don't ask people to in depth questions, somethings are just too personal. With that being said if they wanna talk about deep things then I am open to listening to them. I want people to feel like they trust me before telling me, rather than just telling me because they fill pressured to.

Mike seems to think that because Zak is scared of his brother Mike owns Zak. Like how stupid can you get, are you a child? You don't get to own people. I'm scared of a few people, but not for one minuet do they own me. Honestly, I swear to god Mike is deluded. Mike thinks it's his world and we are all just living in it. I have never met a more arrogant person in my life.

As I mentioned in 'food fight' he asked me out. I thought he was definitely joking, but throughout the week he was deadly serious. It took me a lot by surprise because he didn't know me. He knew what Kacey told him, but that ain't knowing me. So how can he fill like he wants to go out with me. Usually when I date someone, I fancy them or I like how we are together. I am so confused and I should have said no.

Since I was living Redwood, I was at the YMCA every day, so we got to know each other more. I mean I lived 10 minutes down the road. Me, Kacey and Zak would always hang out together. Sometimes with other people from Ym or the kids home, but we would always have a laugh together and nothing was ever taken to seriously. That's what I liked I think, I wsa 15 and I wanted to have a laugh and that's what I was having. I was enjoying myself and managing to get my life back on track at the same time. That's a win, win, I think.

A week since being together he got me the cutest present, it was a teddy and a picture frame of photos of us together. I don't think I had ever been with a boyfriend that was so thought full within a week of knowing each other.

I don't know how long we are going to last, but whilst we are still having a good time its all good. I just can't be bothered with any drama.

Fireworks

Friday the 8th of November was Christchurch fireworks. The kid's home was planning for us all to go. The kids don't usually go out with each other all the time. So, this was the first time in for ever that this has happened. I reckon it's gonna be nice to get to know them properly and by this point me and Sapphire were really close, like how me and Josie was at Woodman's.

We had gotten up to all sorts already and I have only been here a month. Halloween was the night we properly bonded and now we have been doing all nighters. Dancing and singing our life away. We were just having so much fun and she was my best mate at the time. It's crazy how someone can be so important with in a such little time.

Once we had dinner me and Sapphire was getting ready in her room to go out tonight. Yeah, I was only going with the kids home, but you dunno who you are gonna see or what could happen. I don't wear make up all the time, but when I'm going out, I like to make a bit of an effort and I just feel more comfortable when wearing makeup.

Although the annoying thing is Sapphire and Mackenzie have been dating recently and I just find it a bit awkward. Me and Mackenzie use to be a thing and now he's dating my best mate and obviously I want to be happy for her, but I just don't know really how to act when their being very…intimate shall we say.

Mackenzie is really good looking; he has the body of a god and his personality doesn't match his body. You would think someone that is that good looking would be super arrogant and would be a dick, but Mackenzie really ain't like that. He's sweet, kind and generous. I did like him, I know I am dating Zak and Mackenzie is my best mate's boyfriend, but I can't help how I feel. All I can do is not act on how I feel.

When Brooke used to live here, is when me and Mackenzie had a thing. We made out a couple of times and a few more things happened. I probably would have lost me V to him if he had a condom on him. But I think everything happened for a reason.

I love going out with all the kids and some staff from the home. Yes, we ain't family by blood, but we are connected and that makes us kinda like a family. Everyone apart from Mike was going tonight, as he was in London with his boyfriend, I think?

Jay and Trace was taking us tonight, when we usually go out on activities their usually has to be 2 members of staff come if the majority of the house is going and then one has to stay behind. So, because Mike was in London one had to stay behind just in case, he needed to contact staff.

Staff do have a staff mobile, but the majority of the time it isn't charged, doesn't have credit and I don't think all the kids have that number. So, it is just easier if one member stays behind if Mike needs anything.

Also, Kacey was going with Jacob, so I was gonna meet them up there and smoke a fag with them or something. I dunno, because sometimes staff get funny if we go off and do our own thing even though I can be trusted. I will just try and see if I can sneak off for 1 minuet, it's not like I'm meeting a drug dealer, its my sister.

So, the car ride up their; we were blasting out tunes and all having a little sing song. Mackenzie and Sapphire were making out in the boot, which was just too much. I literally hate when people show to much of affection for one another. Also, what was surprising is staff didn't say anything, usually dating in a kid's home wasn't allowed so why is it different for Saph and Kenzie. I think some staff are playing favourites.

When we got there, it was just such a good vibe all around and we were just having banter. It was honestly amazing. I think fireworks night is my favourite time of year. It hasn't always been, but there is just something about it the last couple of years that's made it feel amazing. Sound like such a weirdow right now, but I suppose it's how some people get like when its Christmas or Halloween.

We got their at like 7, but the fireworks weren't until 8ish. So, I met Kacey for a bit and went on some rides. That's kind of mine and Kacey's thing. We love going on fairground rides. Theme Park rides are good and everything, but me and Kacey are like huge pussy's. So that's why we like fair rides so much, because they aren't really that scary and at every fair its pretty much the same rides. Where as in theme parks I think rides vary so much. Also, mine and Kacey's family are poor, so we haven't been able to go to many theme parks in our life.

When it was like 7:45 I went to go find Sapphire and staff as after the fireworks finish it gets crazy packed with everyone trying to leave and I don't think I would have any hope finding them. Which probably means I would be stuck in Ipswich and that was not an ideal situation. So, I said "love you Kace" and off I went to look for them.

The fireworks were amazing as always, Saph and Mackenzie was still like being overly in love with each other. Saph kept trying to get me to dance along with the music and I just didn't want to because it literally felt like everyone was staring at us.

When we got back, I was planning on meeting Zak and Kacey for a fag or something. I hadn't really seen Zak since Halloween, he just made me feel a bit weird and I dunno he didn't make me feel like myself anymore. I feel like with Zak I can't be my out spoken, confident self because he just always puts me down about it. Do I want to be with someone like that? Do I give him the benefit of the doubt? So many questions I need to figure out the answer to.

12 hours in custody

This night was fucked up from the get go, me and Saph shouldn't have kept pushing it the way we did. We should have known when to stop. We just wanted to have banter and a laugh. That's what life should be about, I just don't think staff got the memo.

At 10pm is when the night staff come in. Redwood was very unsettled at the moment, mainly because of me and Saph. So instead of just having 2-night wakes we had to have 3, just in case any thing drastic happened. We have had to have 3-night staff for a while, but the only reason tonight was different was because 2 of the night staff had never been here before. That made me and Saph a little un easy, we didn't like unknown people in our house.

Just before we get into who the 'new' staff was. I just thought I should give you guys a run down of staff and how many we usually have on and that. So, in the morning there is 2 staff on the floor, the manager and usually like a deputy, we have 2 part time deputy's so it varies which one is on. Morning shift is from 6:30-14:30 and management only work 9-5 unless their put on to work in the morning.

Late shift is from 14:30-10:30, which has 3 members of staff on. Also, some times we do have a flexi on, which would be like a normal care worker on an 8-hour shift, but throughout the day, so normally 11-7 or 9-5, it depends what the needs of the home are on that day. Although a flexi is normally on a weekend or school holidays.

Then we have the night wakes. Which I have briefly explained. Their shift runs from 10:30-6.30. some times if we are short staffed than one night wake is replaced with a sleep in.

Crystal primarily works at bury kids home, apparently, she does shifts where ever they need cover. So that could be Woodman's, Lowestoft or Redwood. Tazmin was an agency worker and I know she has never been here before, not even sure if she's worked in a kid's home before. Then alongside both of these clowns was Patricia, she's been working at redwood for like 7 years or something. I dunno, but she has been here a long time.

I know Patricia from when Brooke lived here and I know she didn't like me then. Probably because I wasn't supposed to be in the home, but now I have gotten to know her I think she's amazing.

I know I have said this previously, but you can never say it too much. I don't like new people. They are irrelevant people coming into your life and they all leave eventually. Some you don't understand why they leave and then theirs some people where you almost understand why they leave. Regardless it never gets easier when they do decide to leave. No one or nothing is permanent in your life.

So yeah! Me and Saph were just on one. We did like the cinnamon challenge and the flour challenge which made sapphire puck her guts up. Then things got more out of control. I definitely can't remember who started it, but it escalated more quickly than expected.

I am gonna tell you what I can remember because what I see isn't going to be exactly what Saph sees. Also, we were hyped on adrenaline, so my heart was pounded and things started to go a little blurry. Somehow, we were near the office door, I think we wanted to get in to read our files (this is like our go to thing when shit goes down). Which weren't exactly secure away. They were just on a book shelf in the office. So, anyone could come in and read them. Luckily all the kids here at the moment respect each other's personal shit, I mean we all basically know why we are in here, but without a doubt we don't wanna share all our shit around. Everyone has secrets and so they should.

Staff were pretty sure about not letting us in and that's cool, so Crystal and Tazmin were standing outside whilst Patricia was inside the office and me and Saph were throwing water and washing powder over them. There was way more to it, but I'm not gonna lie at the time it was hilarious and funny. Me and staff were pissing our self's we are just to funny tonight.

Things got a bit crazy when Saph went to go get shit from the kitchen. Like sauces, milk, etc. I was thinking I fucking hope it ain't food fight part 2. It took us hours to clean it last time.

Staff went into the managers office to cool down, which is how me and Saph managed to get in there. Like go cool down outside. In the manager's office there is all the big shit. So, if you want to find anything interesting out about yourself it's gonna be in here. They have these big yellow files, I read some of it at Woodman's, but then staff took it away from mw and I've always wondered what it said. These kinds of files were kept behind a locked door, I was trying to get in it for a very long time, Saph managed to do it straight away. YES SAPH!

I was just sitting at Susan's desk reading my file, what has happened throughout my time with social being involved in my life. Everything since I was 10 years old! In their, there was like a time line, for example; 10 October 2015 I went missing. Basically, my whole life just mapped out in this simplistic form. This just got me more annoyed, why wouldn't they show me this, why would they keep this from me. Surely, I have a write to know what is in my file. I should be allowed to read what is wrote about me regardless of my age.

Susan; she is the homes manager. I think she might have been the only person I didn't know before I moved here. She was replacing the old manager whilst she went on maternity leave. I didn't like Susan much.

Meanwhile Sapphire was going mental, she was slitting her wrists and there was blood pouring out everywhere. She was smashing frames and getting the glass and just cutting herself. I wanted to help, but I didn't think I could, how do you help someone in that situation? I love her, but I don't wanna get hurt for trying to protect her, staff need to get a hold of this because this shit is crazy.

Of course, the police got called, I don't blame the staff because Sapphire was getting so out of control at the moment, I don't think staff even knew what to do at this point. But like I said "it never meant to get this out of hand". It was only supposed to be a laugh.

When the police officer came, I knew him, he use to pick me up when I went missing a lot of times. Although it was surprising because he said to Saph "why can't you be more like this one? She managed to some what turn her life around." I was just thinking that is far from the truth, but I am trying, could be trying harder, but it still matters that I am trying.

Then of course Saph had to dob me in it and I ended up getting nicked for low common assault, which was because I chucked water over someone. Still why the fuck would she dob me in. When even staff didn't say anything about it, I think they didn't want to get me nicked for it because I didn't have that much of an input to the night. They saw it as I made a mistake. The thing is, if I was to blame for the majority of what happened I would never dob my mate in, that's not how I'm built.

But because Saph had brought it up, they couldn't lie about it, especially to a fed. So, they told them exactly what I did, which was just chucking water over someone. Fucking chucking water are they joking.

I have got nicked for a lot of things in my time, I wasn't nicked properly because I was 11,

I think. So they just asked me what happened at my house and then said I had to do community service after school for an hour. Which was litter picking down my road. I was dreading it. The charges were, criminal damage, breaking an entry and theft. It sounds way worse than what it was.

Me and Saph went in a van to bury custody. I manage to sit in the back and Saph was in the cage because she had been self-harming. I think the reason that she dobbed me in, was because she didn't want to go alone. I think she was scared and frightened of just being alone. Her life was going to shit and I think she wanted to bring some one down with her. In this situation it was me.

I think we arrived at bury nick at about 4am, I was so tried and this was my first time being brought to a custody cell, like I didn't know what was gonna happen or what was about to go down. So first of all, they book you in, take names and what happed and all of that, then they pat you down, Saph's had to have a strip search because she was a danger to herself and could be a danger to the police officers. They are literally paranoid about everything; you can't have like those tie things in your trackies and hoodies. If you do, you either have to take them out or they give you other ones to wear. Luckily the only thing I had to give up was my hair band, which was annoying because my hair was very greasy, but I get why they have to be cautious about things and they have to cover for all people that come in here.

I think the last time I was at bury pic was when I had to give a statement about mum and Kacey, I was getting little flash backs and it just made me sad. I'm not gonna tell you what happened because that is Kacey's story to tell.

I asked about my phone call because I know from like movies and that you are allowed one phone call. Of course I was going to call Kacey, I had no one else I wanted to call, also I think she is the only person that is gonna be awake. I mean Zak might be awake, but there is no way I would be calling him up instead of Kacey.

The officer walked me to my cell, but you're not allowed to wear shoes in the cell. I'm not sure why, but your just not allowed. It's not like I even had trainers on, I was wearing uggs. Thank fuck I was wearing socks!

About 10 minutes after I got in my cell the buzzer rang and I spoke through it and they were telling me that my sister was on the other line. I was so glad I had some one to speak to and rant about the whole situation to.

She could not believe when I told her what happened I think she just laughed a lot and was like 'fucking hell'. We spoke for as long as we could, I wasn't sure how long this call was gonna last, but I wanted to make sure I could fit as much stuff as I could into the conversation.

Then I slept and the beds are actually pretty comfy, so much so that when the coppers came in they threatened to keep me in longer when I wouldn't wake up. I am such a deep sleeper, it's not my fault I just really like sleep and I didn't get to sleep until like 6am I reckon. I was so tired.

Then we had the usual, finger prints taken, mug shot taken and then there were the interviews that were taking place. I had to have an appropriate adult because of my age, but it couldn't be a staff member from Redwood because it happened at redwood. They needed someone who wouldn't be a conflict of interest. This all lasted until about 4pm when staff picked us up the next day.

It was just fucking long considering it was because I chucked water over someone. Also, I don't think police are supposed to tell me this, but Saph blamed everything on me. Luckily, they had staff to back me up with what happened, but I genuinely don't how she could do this to me, I thought we were close and loyalty is a massive thing to me. You don't chuck someone you care about under the bus. That's a dick move, snaky little bitch. From now on I am just gonna be cautious about her.

As soon as we got back to Stow, I charged up my phone and I called up Zak and Kacey and I was off again. Didn't even bother getting changed or brush my teeth, although thinking about it now I could of done that whilst my phone was charging. I knew I was having a shower later because my hair was unbearable, so I will just sort shit out then. I just really wanted to see my family.

I met them near Argos, as it was raining and it has a little shelter thing, so we could roll a fag and not get wet whilst doing it. Of course, Zak made it all about him, Kacey wanted to know what had happened and every time I was explaining something Zak would butt in and be like "that never used to be like that when I lived there". Or something like that. He's just getting on my nerves now, this is my story time and I wanna explain shit to my sister. He's supposed to be my boyfriend, be supportive and all that shit. Why can't you just be like that?

Saph's getting kicked out!

After this whole thing, everything's thing been a bit weird at the house. All the kids have been chilled with one another, but the staff seem to be a bit on edge, almost like they are hiding something. Or maybe they are just really upset with what's been going on around the home recently. Whatever it is, it is weird and whatever it is was they weren't telling anyone.

Saph had a meeting with her social worker, Susan and Jenny, to discuss what went down and how to move forward, well at least that's what Saph was told us, but take everything with a pinch of salt.

They completely bombard Saph with getting moved, she had no idea that they were kicking her out on the spot, she thought she would have at least got some warning about it, this ain't right, what they do to kids.

Yeah, the other night we treated staff like shit, yes, we spent the night in a police cell, but we are just kids and we are kids in care. We deserve the respect to be told about our future with enough warning to prepare our emotions. I just really don't understand how the people that care for us can treat us this way.

Whilst we are in their care, it is their responsibility to help us, care for us and listen. They don't have to like us and they can go home to their perfect little lives and forget about us, but whilst they are in my home, they will fucking do what the job description says. Its that fucking simple.

I get why she was getting moved. She is classed as a risk to her and the other people in the home. As the other night, when she was self-harming, it was bad and no words I use can describe how bad it was. That's why she is getting moved and they are going to give me another chance to settle in and make this my home. Saph needs help, more help than this home can give her.

See that's the other reason why I think they want her to move out because me and Saph get along really well and sometimes that means we are bad influences. Personally, I think they want to have a more stable home and that means eliminating the problems so the others can have a chance in achieving what they need to. It sounds harsh and then I didn't get it, but now I get it and I get what it means.

Not only did Saph influence me, but Mackenzie, Robert and even Mike on some occasions, of course I'm not saying she was the only problem because that's not true, but at this moment in time she was the biggest problem and as I said she needs more help than this home can offer her.

I helped her pack a few things, but I didn't know what she wanted where so I was a bit useless. It was sad to see her go and, in all fairness, I didn't make it easy for Jenny to move her. I was blocking her exit, standing in front of her car and even hid some of Saph's things. I was mad, she was my best mate, she made me fit in here and we were like sisters. It was a very sad day I didn't know how to react and all the staff acted like they had no emotion.

She was here for about 3 months I think, so not a huge amount of time, but it was long enough to form bonds and have a relationship with people. How could staff act like they don't give a shit when we are like family here.

Staff just need to have a bit more of respect for the kids that are within the home and the kids that have left. Yes, you get a pay check at the end of the month, but being a good care worker, you should treat us like you would your kids. This ain't to all staff, of course there are some exceptions which are just amazing in every way and they do have emotions and show them, but all staff should be like this! Well in the ideal world they would be, but there's just not enough people that want to do this job with these characteristics.

So Saph was taking her stuff to Jenny's car and as I said I kept hiding things and taking things away, I know she wasn't good for me, but I didn't want her to go. It was weird her and Mackenzie saying bye to each other. They were saying bye like it was the end, even though they are still dating so surely, they would still see one another. I dunno! Like I said "weird".

Then when I finally move away from the car, I saw her get in it and I literally just felt like crying their and then, but I didn't. Throughout my time in care, I have seen so many social workers, foster carers, care workers, foster kids, kids of foster parents leave and it still never gets easier because like it or not I care about people. That is my weakness, I always care to much about people. They can fuck me over at least 10 times before I tell them to fuck off. I act like I don't care, but what I do and what I feel like is 2 very different things. It is very easy for people to put on a façade, I should know I do it all the time!

Just like that Saph was gone, it was an end of an era, I was the only girl in a house full of boys. I have never lived with just boys. I don't even have a brother, so I have no idea how the rest of my time in this house is going to pan out. Saph was literally the only thing keeping me sane. Being the only girls, we had things in common, had things to talk about. Yes, I was close with the boys, but they are always gonna be closer with each other than me.

A few months later… Robert told me something. I didn't know how to act and I asked if it was when Mackenzie and Saph were together. He didn't answer that so I assumed it was. Robert and Saph fucked, in Robert's bed, I don't know how they kept this a secret. These 2 are the biggest loud mouths I know. Robert had to tell Mackenzie because Mackenzie and Saph are still a thing, I think. Robert told Mackenzie and Mackenzie ended it.

Brody moves in

So, we all knew this was gonna happen eventually, I guess we just didn't expect how soon. It has literally only been about 3 weeks and there are already talks about another kid moving in. I don't ever wanna be bitch to a kid that needs a home, but at the same time we are finally being closer as a home and now you wanna throw another child into the mix. Like how is that fair on any of us kids.

The thing is, is they don't even tell us till like a few days before their coming to look round. Also, they don't really tell us anything about them. We have house meetings about once a week, usually on Thursdays and these are there to discuss what's going on in the home, if there any changes that are happening. You don't have to attended but they prefer you to go, so you don't miss out on important things. Also, we usually get a take away after for attending.

This is when we found out Brody was going to come for visit, we found out his name (Brody), we found out his age (12) and that was basically it. We didn't find anything about what he was like, what he was into, we were basically meeting him blind.

I get there are some things you can't tell us because of confidentiality reasons, but there must be some things you can tell us to help prepare us for him being a part of the home. I dunno, I think it's important for the rest of us. I get it is a kid's home, but this is still our home and we deserve what kind of an impact this is going to have. Decisions are being made that will have an impact of the home and I think we deserve to be apart of the conversation at least.

So, the day came where Brody was going to have a look round and have dinner basically like what I did. First impressions of him, well he seemed very quiet, he had his hood up and literally just walked past all of us.

Me and Rob was sitting at the breakfast bar, when Brody and I think his social worker walked in through the back door. That's what I mean by he walked straight past us, it was only until I said hi, did he say hi.

I get why he would be shy because he's 12. He's moving in to a house full of 4 other kids, about 20 members of staff. I was nervous looking round here and I still knew basically everyone from here. It's a nerve-wracking experience to any one especially a little kid.

So usually when a kid moves in or there are talks about them moving in, they come for a look round and has dinner. Then they usually try and have them stay for one night. So, they get to meet the night staff, also they get to see if their okay and comfortable at night time I guess. The only reason this didn't happen to me was because I already was at a children's home and they are basically the same, but also because when I moved in woodman's was going to close down. There wasn't time.

With little kids or more shy kids this is a really great opportunity because they get to see how the house works. When I moved it too Woodman's, Josie basically threatened to beat me up, when I first walked in the door, but that's another story.

Regardless of whether you like it or not this is where you are going to be living, unless you are in danger, they ain't going to change it. They say it's for your benefit and I suppose it kind of is, but at the same time you don't get a choice. As there is to many kids and not enough social workers, for all the social workers to care. Social workers just want an easy life and to get you settled as soon as possible.

So yeah, we were all like on our best behaviour and I wanted to try and make him as comfortable as possible. So, I tried to make conversation, but he literally said one-word answers. He isn't a chatty one, which I guess is good? Robert does enough chatting for fucking everybody.

The relationship

So, I know this may be a bit of a jump from Brody moving in, but Mine and Zak's relationship was a huge part of me living at Redwood. We got together on the 7th October 2016 and broke up on the 2nd March 2017. So, we weren't together a mad amount of time, but it was long enough for me to love him. It was long enough for him to manipulate me and give me a massive head fuck.

I am not gonna sit here and say our whole relationship was shit and I was miserable all the time because it wasn't. For the first 2 months I think, it was good he spent Christmas with my family, we hung out like every day, he was there in my corner cheering me on with whatever I chose to do and I needed that I needed for someone to say their permanent. My whole life I have had people dipping in and out of my childhood, school and my time in care.

Then when he got kicked out of the YM and when he got his own flat he did he get more weird and controlling. He was a horny teenager all the time, he just wanted was sex and when I didn't want to he would cheated on me. Being cheated on is the worst feeling, it makes you feel like you are not good enough, it makes you feel disgusted with your body! It just makes you wonder what you did wrong.

So, when I use to go round to his place, without a doubt he would want something. Same as when we stayed round my mums, I didn't know whether he just valued me as a human sex doll. Yes, you are right, I didn't have to have sex with him, that was my choice, but when you are alone with that person in a house, at least 15 minutes walking away from where you live, with a man who is a lot stronger than you, it's difficult to say no out of fear of what could happen. Sometimes I didn't feel like I had a choice, that choice was taken away from me.

One night at his I think I turned him down like 10 maybe 12 times. He kept trying to make a move and I kept telling him to back the fuck off. Like I didn't wanna have sex for like one day, I just couldn't be bothered. But he kept coming back and making a move, trying to reach down my trousers or trying to go under my shirt. By the 10th time I literally felt like okay, if I turn him down again, is he going to rape me? Every time I said go away, he got pissed and came back even stronger. I know you all are probably thinking why didn't I just walk out, I'm strong, but not strong enough. I stayed because of fear. Fear of the unknown?

Our relationship got toxic as soon as he got his 'job', I put it in quotation marks because it wasn't a job. He didn't get paid for it, all he did was help his mate out and this is when he started cheating on me. He started hanging around this group of people who are not even worth a mention, he took this girl back to his place and fuck knows what went down. I know this because he told Kacey he kissed another girl. Was he bragging? Why did he tell my sister? The one person who was guaranteed to tell me. That's where the mind games come into it.

Then when he came down the back of redwood that day I asked him about it, I said why would my sister lie? She doesn't gain anything out of this relationship. He had the audacity to break up with me because I was and I quote 'being a dumb slut'. Then he just walked off. I went running up the road after him because I loved him and it was that simple. He came running back the next day and I forgave him like a fucking idiot, I look back and think why would I take him back, he gave me a way out, he dumped me, but like I said I was in love with him. I was young and I did just want someone to love me.

The second time he broke up with me was because I was focused on school work, by this time I was getting home schooled and I had tutors 3 times a week at the Mix. I wanted to do well. Social tried to make me to re take year 10 as I was only, their for 2 weeks out of the whole entire school year. I wanted to make people proud and prove them wrong. I was so ready to turn my life around, it might have been a little bit late, but better late than never.

After my tutor session, he walked me back to redwood and we got into an argument for something I can't remember because it was stupid and completely his fault. But he said straight to my face "fuck you we are done."

The last and final time we broke up was because I was gonna stay round Kacey's for like the first time, as I only just turned 16 and I was only just allowed to. Zak didn't like I was gonna stay round Kacey's and not his. He met me at Redwood, he said he was gonna walk me up to the Ym which I appreciated. I mean it was late and I would have liked to spend more time with him before I go there. Just because I wanted to stay round Kacey's doesn't mean I didn't wanna spend time with him.

On the way up there we didn't really speak, we only spoke to when we were like 30 seconds away from the Ym and I think he just spoke then to stop me going to see Kacey. Even then it wasn't a good chat. He started getting loud and in my face. I finally got the strength to get back up in his face and say "get in my face one more time!" and then I said "I don't need to put up with this shit, fuck you and fuck off I am done."

Of course, he did his usual thing and walk off and call me a slag. Even though he's the second guy I have slept with.

Later that night, he tried to worm his way back in, but I weren't having none of it, I dunno if it was because I had Kacey with me or if I just felt weight of my shoulders. Whatever it was I was glad it was over.

The next day when I came back to redwood. Zak came by again. He wanted to speak to me, so we went outside and sat on the wall, on the side of the house and he said " I want you back Immie, I don't want anyone else apart from you." This guy, sitting right in front of me now is the guy I fell in love with, he was actually having a Propper conversation with me, he was being genuine and he seemed like he cared.

However, the last 2 months I can't forget, I just can't. I fell in love with person I am seeing right now. I didn't fall in love with a cheat, a liar, a sexual predator and those things are who Zak had become. I deserve better.

Zak was my first Propper relationship, I have loved before, I loved Ryan at Woodman's, but that was a different kind of love. The way I loved Ryan was because he was so hot, he would do anything for me, but I pushed him away because that is the kind of person I am or who I was at the time.

The way I loved Zak, was raw. It had arguments; it was toxic. I didn't feel the same way about Ryan as I did Zak. It was hard to look Zak in the face and say I didn't wanna be with him anymore and whilst I was doing this, all I saw was how I broke up with Ryan because it is basically the same. Apart from Ryan was a decent guy and didn't have a bad bone in his body.

I needed to put this relationship in the book now because it affected me in many ways. I was 15/16 years old. At 16 in the eyes of the care system you are deemed an adult. I knew this relationship was not how I wanted to start 'adult life' I knew if I didn't get out now when would I be able to. I wanted to get a job, get good grades, I moved to Redwood because I wanted a fresh start not still be doing all the childish stuff I once did.

And I am glad I got out because in 2018 he got arrested for assaulting 63-year-old homeless women and leaving her for dead. He's currently serving a 12-year sentence behind bars.

Also, I have never gone in depth about this relationship because until now I wasn't ready. This book is therapy to me. Putting all my feelings, emotions and actions on paper, it's like I can finally put it to bed.

Mike is leaving

Mike never really was at redwood when I moved there, I knew him from when Brooke use to live here. That's when we really started to form a friendship because we use to hang out all the time.

Although that was about a year ago, he had grown up a lot since then. He is more cocky and very full of himself. He had to and needed to be the best. He never liked the thought that anyone could be better than him and when someone appeared more smarter than him, he turned vile.

Although he can be very sweet and thought full like when I first moved in there, he offered to help me move my stuff in and he did it without hesitation.

The more I continued to stay at Redwood, the more I started to see Mike's true colours and who he actually really was. He is very clever and with that he is able to manipulate the situation, but I didn't really live with him for that long.

About a year ago I think or 6 months ago, he went missing for 2 weeks, I think. I am not sure, but it was a long time to get people really worried about him. It turns out that actually he was in London for the majority of the time, I can't remember the fine details and I don't wanna insult Mike and make up something that just isn't true, but also that would be his story to tell.

He wanted to move out of Redwood to live with his boyfriend who lives in London and with him being 16 he is able to, as in the eyes of social he's an adult. I think it would be the best decision for him at this current time, I mean he isn't really their anyways so now he can spend as much time as he can with him.

I moved in in the September and his birthday is in November, I think by the time I moved in he didn't really care about Redwood, he knew he was going to be out of here soon. So, he wanted to have a laugh here whilst he still could.

He spent most of his time in London on the weekends and when he was here during the week, he literally went to school and that was pretty much it, well and causing shit.

Even though I said all those things about Mike at the start, he is very loyal and he does stick up for his own. So, if he respects you and cares about you then you have always got some one fighting in your corner.

On the week of him moving out he stayed at redwood a lot more. He's been living at Redwood for at least a year or something like that, that's a long time to build relationships with people. They have been his carers for a long time, moving out of a placement is hard especially if you like living there. It's annoying because we all have to move out of some time and if we don't move out on our own, then the day before we turn 18, they will kick you out anyway. So, it's always best to go somewhere you want to.

Me and Robert helped Mike sort his room out the best we could, we didn't want to be to invasive. But what we wanted to help because we are all like a family in here and the last couple of months Sapphire has left and Brody has moved in and now Mike is leaving as well. Now there will be only me, Robert and Mackenzie that are the original bunch.

About a day before Mike was leaving, he wrote us all cards, kids and staff. I thought it was so sweet and each and every card was different. They were personal to us; they symbolised the journey we had been on. It was very sweet and very special!

On the morning of him moving he had to leave really early as they had a long drive ahead of them. So, we said our final good byes and off he went. Just like that, slightly emotional, but it's what happens, when you live in care. I was very surprised I was up that early to see Mike off.

Christmas time.

This Christmas I was going to spend at home, with Kacey, mum, mum's boyfriend and Zak. I was so excited this is the first Christmas I had spent at home in 3 years. I just couldn't wait we were gonna sleep over and hopefully get drunk and just have a really good time. I am very excited.

Before that, Redwood was planning a Christmas meal, where we were all gonna go out to the hungry horse in Claydon and hopefully have a really nice meal. Some staff that weren't even working were gonna come along, I could just tell it was gonna be amazing. We were planning to do a secret Santa. So, everyone that was coming picked a name out of a hat. I pulled Christophers name out.

I literally had no idea what I was going to get him, the budget was £5 given to us by the kids home, so I couldn't just give him the money I had to actually get him a present. I have never had to by a guy a present that had a budget on it. Also, guys that have a 'professional' relationship with you is very difficult to buy for. As you could get him a 'funny' present, but then do you cross that line of professionalism?

So, when we were getting our snack box in Tesco's, I saw something and I was like that is what I want to get him. It was Thorntons chocolate in the shape of a football and it was only £4.

He loved football; he supports Liverpool. I always use to make jokes about how Liverpool are shit like; what's the difference between a tea bag and Liverpool… the tea bag stays in the cup longer. Or what's the difference between a McDonalds milkshake and Liverpool fans…nothing their both thick as shit.

Christopher was part of my key team. We had a very good relationship and we just got on, he also had my back and supported me a lot. His wife actually worked at Woodman's. He was amazing and I don't think I could say a bad thing about him. Of course, we had disagreements, but they were not like arguments. Just heated conversations and I think they mostly happened because he could see my potential and I didn't want to let him down. I never want to let anyone down.

I am slightly curious as to who has gotten me because if it's another kid, they ain't going to have a clue on what I want or even what to get me, but I suppose it's all for fun really. Still want a good present though.

The day of the meal arrived; we all met at the hungry horse. Our meals were already pre ordered, so we just got to sit down, got the drinks in. It was so good to be out of the home having a nice meal with more than 3 members of staff. We actually just felt like a family. It was surprising how many staff actually came on their day off.

It is just so nice to be able to have most of the staff and all of the kids out. This was the first time that we all got to do this as a whole. In this moment we just felt united.

So much shit gets talked about being in a kid's home, but the reality is, its one of the best memories I have. Living in care is lucky, I am able to have such a big support network and for that I am forever grateful.

Before we had the food to come out, we all exchanged secret Santa gifts. I got the cutest thing. So, at this moment in my life, I was addicted to Dr pepper, like that is literally all I use to drink and Tinisha use to be so mad about it. It was only because she cared, but she use to say how bad it was for your teeth, that you can gain a lot of weight from drinking it. I got it, but I still loved it.

Anyway, I got 2 bottles of Dr pepper, one was full, like a normal Dr pepper you would buy from the shop. The other one was full of coke bottles. The sweets you get from the shop. I had an inkling who got this for me, I thought it was Susan. 2 reasons, because everyone else had kinda already guessed who's their gifts were from. Also, it seemed like a gift that she would have gotten me. I said "thank you" around the table because I could have been wrong.

When Christopher opened his gift, he was shocked and happy. He didn't believe it only cost £4. I admitted it was me, even though it wasn't part of the game, but I wanted to make sure that he knew it was literally under budget. He was very grateful for it and he said "I am sure my wife will help me eat this".

The food was amazing, I can't remember exactly what I had, but I am pretty sure that I had a burger and a chocolate brownie. Just because that is like my go to whenever I go out to a pub or restaurant.

So, me, Kacey and Zak were all gonna go down mums on Christmas eve and come back on boxing day. Jacob always has Christmas at his nans that's why he wasn't gonna come down, but Kacey was going to spend boxing day or the 27th round with his family.

I was so excited! My first Christmas with my boyfriend and I'm so glad he gets along so well with my family. Also, this was going to be the first Christmas me or Kacey has spent with Joe (mum's boyfriend) as their relationship was kind of new.

Mum picked us all up outside of Ym, we all got a little tipsy on Christmas eve and had a good night. Later that night when mum and Joe was both upstairs Zak tried to have sex with me. I literally straight up refused. Let's just back up a little bit...

What use to be mine and Kacey's room is now just a storage place. They have got a bed in there, but there is literally no room for us to sleep in there, also there is just one bed, instead of the 2 that was their when we lived here so one of us would have to sleep on the sofa any ways.

Also, my mums house is just so messy, like there was a reason I went into care. The fact is, it wasn't just messy, it was dirty which made it worse. I think I am just glad that Zak didn't really care what my mums house looked like.

We just all agreed to sleep down stairs. Mum has a leather corner sofa and a 2-seater sofa. Me and Zak slept on the corner sofa and Kacey slept on the 2 seater sofa. This is why I didn't wanna have sex with him. I am not gonna have sex with Zak when my sister is like less than 10 meters away. She is still awake; she would hear everything and that is just messed up. We are close, but not that close.

Zak still kept trying and I just got up this courage to put my foot down and said no. Like I wasn't having any of it. I knew here was a safe place and Kacey would stick up for me and would make my voice herd. I'm her little sister, she would do anything to protect me.

IT'S CHRISTMAS!!! We all opened presents and then had Christmas lunch, we usually always have like a big roast dinner at lunch time and then in the evening we will have left overs or like snacky type things. That's always what we use to do at Gran and Grandads.

The roast was good, but it wasn't like the one we use to have at Gran and Grandads when we were younger. Mostly because most things weren't made from scratch and I hate frozen roast potatoes.

Although I am just being picky, mum tried and that's what counts. It's not fair to compare her Christmas day to Grans. Grans been alive a lot longer than mum has; nothing beats your Grans cooking.

It was just a really chilled out day, I got a little bit drunk, but that's what Christmas was all about. Being here with family and actually spending time with people that matter for a change. Even though I am home, it doesn't really feel like home any more.

I feel like mum hasn't made space for us if either of us did want to move back home. Like we don't even have our own room any more, we have to sleep on the sofa. It's just sad, it looks like home, but home is where the heart is and this just isn't it any more. Redwood is my home; Redwood is where my heart is.

When it was bed time Zak got pissed off for some reason and said he was gonna sleep on a chair in the kitchen. Me and Kacey was just pissing ourselves because it was funny, this whole night was funny. Zak was getting pissed for no reason and literally was just being a complete and utter dick.

Like why the fuck would you wanna sleep in the kitchen, it's a bit weird. Although at this point, I would just like to say, it wasn't a kitchen chair. For some reason mum had like an armchair in the kitchen and that's where he wanted to sleep.

About not even 5 minuets later me and Kacey saw him come back in and get on the corner sofa. We both said "did you not wanna sleep in the kitchen anymore."

He just replied with "no it was cold". Me and Kacey just couldn't help our self's, but we just started crying with laughter. Zak got pissed again and went for a fag. We felt bad, but it was funny.

We came back early on boxing day morning, I say early, it was early for us and I say morning it was more like lunch time. We stopped and got a Maccer's on the way back. They dropped me off first and then went to the Ym and dropped Kacey and Zak off.

It was a good couple of days and probably the best days I have had in a while, but I am glad to be back home. I have enjoyed the last couple of days, but it is good to be back to where my real home is.

New year

After Christmas, always brings a new year. With a new year brings new hope. At least that is what I have always believed. But I think it is true, I have always looked to a new year and been hopeful about it because I hope this year would bring my life back on track.

I always set resolutions, I hardly ever keep to them, so not sure why I still bother. They're usually the same shit any way. Keep saying I am going to quit smoking for the past 2 years and I haven't actually managed to achieve it yet. One year I will achieve it!

This year I am going to give myself, what I believe to be manageable things to do. I wanna study hard so I am able to get decent GCSE results, I wanna get a job so I have my own money and I don't have to keep relying on pocket money staff give me. I want the year 2017 to mean something in my life, I want this year to be the year I get recognised and noticed.

This new year I was gonna go down mums again and Zak was gonna come down with me. Kacey, Jacob were gonna go out with his family, to like their local pub, I think. I was excited to see the new year in with Zak and mum. I wouldn't wanna spend it with anyone else and mum allows me to drink so I will be getting drunk tonight. Getting drunk and having fun is what the new year is all about.

When I was younger me, Kacey and mum would spend new year's at gran and grandads. Little bit like Christmas. I would usually pass out about 10 in the lounge and they would have to carry me upstairs to bed. I always tried to stay up and see the new year in, but could never manage it.

I use to love sleeping at Gran and grandads, we use to sleep in mum's old room. Me and Kacey always shared a room at Gran and Grandads. Gran would always put a hot water bottle in our bed so it would warm up because their house is usually freezing.

I only started staying up past 12am from when I was about 10, doesn't seem that old, but I had a different life to other 10-year-old kids, 10 years old for me was like 14. I have made new year resolution's since I can remember, when I was younger, I would write them down with my Gran and mum. Now I just kinda make a mental note in my head of how I can improve myself for a better year than the last. No one is perfect and I believe there is always room for improvement.

Anyway, mum picked me and Zak up and we went to Tesco's before we went back to mums, Tesco's is literally right round the corner from mums. Then we literally just chilled, me and Zak went for a walk and I showed him places I use to go as a kid, but of course somehow, he seemed to make it all about him. I dunno how, but that is just what Zak does, its literally like his talent.

I never use to like Sudbury when I was little because that was really all I knew. The people down Sudbury weren't nice and it just seemed like a really toxic place, but now I love going back down there and seeing where I use to spend most of my time and just really good child memories.

It was nice seeing mum and spending time down there, but there was literally nothing to do. It was slightly boring, but Zak seemed to enjoy himself somehow. We just watched the BBC fireworks that are always broadcasted, we drank and then went to bed. That was literally our night. It was boring without Kacey down here.

The next day about 12, mum drove us back literally like last time. Also, we stopped and got a Maccers on the way home. There isn't a Maccers in stow, so whenever I came to Sudbury, I always wanted to get one. Most of the time mum would pay, but sometimes they would make me pay. Mum also use to charge me for petrol money. Which I think is slightly out of order! I think mum thinks I am made of money, but the only money I get is pocket money and my incentive money.

In a kid's home you do get money, they have to give it to you by law, I think. However, you have certain achievements you have to do in order to receive it. For example, you get your pocket money if you have tidied your room. Your pocket money you get it every week, but you don't have to tidy your room every week. As your pocket money will just build up. Pocket money varies for each age. I was 15 so I got £4.50, I think.

The other way you are able to get money is by incentives. You are able to set your incentives to whatever you want to. You have 2 incentives, one which is 7 days and one that is 5 days. You don't have to do this, you just won't get a tick for that day, which means you will have to wait longer for that £5. So, mine was go to bed by 11pm every night, I didn't have to be asleep by then I just had to be in my room. To go to education when I had it, if I didn't have it on one day then I still had to do revision at home.

It was pretty decent because if you did what you were supposed to do, you could earn like £15 in a week.

So far so good!

2017 has been pretty decent so far. Jill from red rose chain contacted me about making my book into a play. Last year there was talks about it and I actually met Jill and I am so excited that its actually happening and that it's not just talk! Dreams do actually come true!

I am having regular meetings to discuss how my book can be transformed into a play, it's also being funded and commissioned by Suffolk County council. I am just very excited with it all and cannot wait for the process to begin. I can't believe this is happening to me, this kinda thing never happens to me.

Also, it is official, I am no longer in school. Kez grave said about a managed move, the only problem with that is, is that I am in year 11 and about to take my GCSE's and there is just no point to starting a new school. I would be leaving in a couple of months. I don't think any other school would take me, especially with my record.

I am having lessons at the Mix 3 times a week, Maths, English and science. These are only going to be for 2 hours max, the rest of the time I am going to be revising out of a text book and the tutors will be setting me home work and stuff like that. I think this would better for me, I have never really fitted in well with school. Mostly because I always move around and can't be bothered to make friends or even try and fit in. then if I don't have any friends, I will be called every name possible. I think home schooling will be a great decision as long as I can stay focused.

I think a good thing about being home schooled is that I will be able to learn at my own pace and I will be able to focus on what I need to do in order to pass my GCSE's. I need to prove to a lot of people that I am able to do this.

On not so good news, some new staff are starting at Redwood. I don't like new people in my life, especially people I don't care about and have no interest in caring about. They are probably gonna be here for a month at best and then fuck off again. A lot of people aren't cut out for this job.

There was this one woman, Beatrice, she is very out spoken and for a new member of staff very confident and makes herself at home. I don't like her, she is coming into my home and making it hers. Maybe it's a good thing, but I can't see it yet.

A women name Bianca is starting as well, she seems strict, but not strict without reason. Very very crazy personality, but the truth is I am not sure how I feel about her either of them at the moment.

Like I said "I don't like new members of staff" or just new people in fact, that's down to my issues and I recognise that. I shouldn't be mean them because their new, they might actually like what the job is about, but what I am gonna hate it is, is their coming into this job thinking one thing and leaving 2 weeks later. It's a kid's home, it's not gonna be all sunshine's and rainbows. These are real kids with real problems, this ain't no Tracey beaker shit or the dumping ground.

I get redwood has to hire more staff members, otherwise there would be no kid's homes, but I personally think that their hiring process could do with some adjusting. I think the kids having an input into the interviews could change a lot.

For one the kids can feel at eased with them being hired, they could also give feedback to the managers on if they think they would be best suited for the job. I am not saying that the kids should dictate who gets hired, but who knows the home better than the kids that actually are living there.

Zak has been doing my head in, hes getting kicked out of the Ym, but he hasn't got any where to go. I think there were talks about him going to live with Tyrone at his flat, Tyrone moved out of Ym like last year I think, but Zak knew him from when they both lived at Redwood.

For whoever knows me, when I am in a relationship, yes, I like to hang out with my boyfriend and that, but I hate someone being very needy, it kinda puts me off them. I like to have my own space and I like to have breathing room. I don't have to meet up with him every day because some days I wanna just chill or I wanna just meet my sister. And most of all I shouldn't have to explain myself if I don't wanna meet him. Because that is my decision and he should just allow what the fuck I say.

When he does officially move out of Ym it will be harder to split my time I reckon because he's going to be living on the opposite side of Stowmarket. So, whoever I choose to spend my time with the other one ain't going to be very happy.

Just before the new year all the staff that were over here from Woodman's are now heading back to Woodman's as they have reopened and have to do some training before they have kids living their again. When I actually left Woodman's, it was hard because I loved all the staff their and to me that was my family. But I accepted it and I managed to say good bye because I knew I would still see some of them at Redwood.

However, I actually have to say bye now. The person I was so sad at saying bye to was Elvis because he has helped me through so much and for everything, he does and did I am so so grateful. Elvis is one in a million, no one and nothing can ever replace Elvis.

I was a little sceptical about having him as a key worker at Woodman's because I don't get along with guy role models very well, mainly because I haven't really had my dad be a big apart of my life until recently. Although when I got to Elvis and all the key work sessions we had together, he is legit like my grandad. I could type all the amazing things about Elvis, but I am pretty sure that's not why you guys are reading this book (Elvis might disagree with that statement though, he would love to read about his amazing qualities).

As well as Elvis leaving Jay, my current key worker is also leaving. To be fair to him, the reason for him leaving is because he wanted to help kids in another way. Which to be honest I think is pretty sweet of him, he does do this job because he cares, even though he probably got the job because of his mum.

So that means I will be getting a knew key worker. I just really hope it is not a new member of staff. Tinisha doesn't have a key child at the moment and me and her get along really well, she is legit like my older sister, but once again us kids don't get to decide who it is! Even though I think this we should be allowed to, within reason, but we still should get a say. After all this is our life!

So far, I have managed to do what I wanted to do with my 2017. I am not gonna start and say I am perfect because I know I am not, but I think I am doing alright so far.

Beatrice!!!

Beatrice, Beatrice, Beatrice, so yeah, its official one of the new members of staff is my new key worker. As you can tell this news was a little bit of a shock, I mean, it's a little bit un fair when I have explicitly expressed my feelings towards new people having an input in my life. Yet, here we are.

It's like they haven't taken my feelings into consideration at all. Beatrice has a better relationship with Robert and Mackenzie than me. I just think they have done this on purpose, it's not like I didn't make my voice herd.

I know it wasn't Beatrice's fault, she didn't do anything to me not to like her, it was as simple as her being new in my house. I felt bad that I put up a guard towards her when all she was trying to do was help kids in this house.

When she became my key worker, we had to go on key work times together, I mean I didn't have to go with her, I could of chosen to go with Christopher, but she was my keyworker, I felt slightly obligated to give her a chance. And well if she blows that, at least it is not my fault any more.

I came back from staying at my mums and I had just had my tongue pierced. So, people could barely understand what the fuck I was saying, I had to keep repeating what I was saying over and over again. I also gained a slight lisp which was just hilarious to Robert.

Any one that who has ever got their tongue pierced, knows it hurts so much, but the after care is so much worse. You don't really understand how much you use your tongue for until you can't actually use it.

So yeah, me and Beatrice was going to have some key time, we went to Maccers at white house, Ipswich. I have no idea why I chose to go to Maccers because I knew it would hurt to eat, I was just really really hungry and I love Maccers so much, if you couldn't tell. Usually, I get a burger or something, but I was trying to think of something that's easier to eat, so I went with chicken nuggets. Took me half an hour to eat and I didn't manage to finish the fries as they were just cold by the end of it, but that time allowed me and Beatrice to get to know each other.

She was doing most of the talking because I couldn't eat and talk. It just wasn't gonna happen, so I was asking her questions about what she's like, what she use to do before. I wanted to give her a chance because she did actually seem alright.

After getting to know her some more I felt more confident about our relationship moving forward. To me it is a big deal about having a good relationship with my key worker because I need to have a good relationship with them in order to be able to share things with them. I had a good relationship with Elvis, Jay and now hopefully Beatrice.

After this keywork session me and Beatrice basically became in separable, we ended up having a really close bond, which is strange considering I didn't wanna no her at first. I was able to let her in and that's one of the best decisions I ever made.

She always use to come to town with me late at night to meet Kacey and Zak. Our longest key work time was 3 and half hours, which is ridiculously long. On that key work time we were playing pool and just chatting a load of shit basically. The best thing about this was is Beatrice treated me like her daughter. She was the mum I needed.

Beatrice didn't just see a label on me, when she looked at me, she didn't think care kid. She thought that I was someone who hadn't been loved properly, hadn't been cared for and she wanted to be a part of that process.

There is nothing bad now I can say about her, I love her like she is my own mum. She has done so so much for me, I am not going to tell them all now, so you will have to keep reading to find out more. But honestly, I don't say this often, but I was very very wrong about my first impression of Beatrice. Who I now call Nanny.

I started calling her nanny because we went to cop dock Tesco's and I was basically like technically you are old enough to be my nan. She replied with 'if I had a daughter at 15 and she had a daughter at 15 then you are right. So, if me and my daughter was a slag then you could be.'

I called her nanny all around Tesco's, she was so embarrassed, mostly because she has never been called nanny before and she doesn't look as old as she is. She is 45, but honestly, she looks like 38. Like she ages pretty well and she doesn't act like she's 45 either she is a cool mum and now an even cooler nanny.

We have had so many laughs together and I am actually so grateful for what she has done and continues to do for me.

I will tell you guys more things of what we have been up to as the story goes on, but nanny had my back and that is what I needed. A member of staff actually sticking up for me, but also if she thinks I am wrong she will say that. Because that is just what makes her amazing.

The Tesco's trip

Going to Tesco's is always funny with the home. If you don't know, we use to always go to Tesco's once a week because we get these things called snack boxes. Which is basically £5 that we get to spend on any crips, chocolate, drinks, for the week. As you don't get to buy unhealthy stuff on the shopping list, I might of mentions snack boxes before, but just in case here it is.

We don't have to space it out throughout the week, but once it was gone it was gone and we wouldn't get any more until next week, unless of course we chose to buy it with our own money. Snack boxes are usually done on a Monday because then we can remember when we have to get it next. Although if you can't get it on the Monday you are able to get it on the Tuesday, but if you just cant be bothered to go then you will loose out on it.

Although this chapter isn't actually about the snack box. A Tesco's trip is always funny, I think their funnier when you go their late at night, or if you go their drunk. Well, I thought that until this Tesco's trip.

Tilly needed to go to Tesco's and I said I would go with her because I had finished all my lessons for the day and I was just bored to be honest. During the week, we are only allowed wifi after school hours. It's like an incentive to go to school I think, although online lessons are excluded from this. So usually when I do have an online lesson, I take advantage of the wifi being on.

I would rather walk round Tesco's than stay here, literally doing nothing and not being able to talk to anyone, or watch Netflix. Also, just because I can meet Kacey and Zak all the time doesn't mean I want to. Like I love them with all my heart, but sometimes immie needs her own space.

So yeah, off me and Tilly went, we had to get a few things that were missed off the shopping list. I am not sure why we didn't go to Lidl, but I weren't paying so I didn't really care where we went.

Also, this may be relevant or it may not be, but it is important for it to be put out there and for some reason I thought it was important at the time. Tilly was dressed in comphys. Full track suit, messy hair, obviously there is nothing wrong with this, but it helps paint a picture of maybe why tilly was embarrassed by the end of this shopping experience and maybe why she was questioned a bit more!

We were just casually going down the aisles, getting what we need and I was just in a really funny mood, when I am funny, I'm hilarious and when I'm not I am just boring. There is just no in between with me. Honestly sometimes I think I am boarder line bipolar.

I was making snide comments with Tilly, me and tilly have really good banter. Tilly is decent and she doesn't take what I say to personally and she just comes back with similar remarks. When we got to the check out, I was saying to the checkout lady "help, they lock me in my room, you need to help me". All this shit.

Whilst I was saying all of this, Tilly was just packing up the bags going bright red and she didn't know what to say. She didn't have an id badge with her and I mean she didn't really have any leg to stand on. You could see it in her face, what she was thinking. She kept eye rolling me, wishing I would just shut the fuck up.

My favourite card to play is the care kid card and I am very good at playing it. Care kids get so down about being in care that they forget that it can use it to your advantage. Tilly knew all of this was a joke and of course nothing would actually happen to her and it was just a joke. As long as Tilly knew that then I was fine because if it was any other staff member, they probably would actually lock me in my room and not feed me for a week (also a joke- kinda). Just some staff members seem to take life to seriously and with this job only be serious when you need to.

Although the checkout lady looked a little scared, but because Tilly was laughing, she didn't take it too far. However, security basically followed us to the car and made sure everything was actually okay.

How tilly was dressed and the fact that she didn't have her id badge and also because Tilly does look young for how old she is, didn't really go in her favour.

To this day we still laugh about it and because of this she always carries her badge with her all the time now.

This chapter isn't very long and its was defiantly way funnier at the time than it is now. I feel like chapter was important to include because it shows the funnier side of being in a kid's home and how well staff and the kids get on.

New kid alert

As you probably know by now, people come and go from a kid's home and new kids move in. Redwood is always getting referrals with kids that need some where to go and they have to do a risk assessment, to see the risks regarding the other kids in the home, also they do it to see if they would fit in every one in the home.

So, a new guy came for dinner just like Brody did, same as before we didn't know anything about him, only his name. He is called Brandon. This time we knew even less about him, the next one I don't even think we are gonna get his name.

When he first walked in the door, he seemed chilled, although he did wanna fit in and he was a little strange. He was wearing this hat, like a proper gentleman's hat, not a roadman hat, a shirt and smart jeans. He looked like he's made a proper effort. He is 14 I think he said? He's from Lowestoft. So same place as Robert.

He hit it off with the guys instantly, I mean of course he would. I am the only girl and he didn't know how to talk to me and that was okay. I wasn't going to pressure him to feel like he had to speak to me. I could tell he had autism or was at least on the spectrum, that didn't make me treat him differently, it just made me be more considerate how I might explain things.

He wanted to fit in because he went out side with us and asked for a fag. I know I started smoking young and I was only 15 now, but I don't give fags to people who are young and also people who also don't smoke.

He didn't need to smoke, it's not cool and it doesn't make you fit in. It just leaves you with dirty lungs and barely able to run to catch a bus. Bottom line is, I started because I thought it was cool and 5 years late, I seriously regret it. If I could quit I would, but I'm addicted.

I think he wasn't going to stay one night because it was pretty much definite that he was going to move in. He just wanted to come and have a look around. It was just really far away for him. His home, school, friends, everything was in Lowestoft. So, I kinda feel bad for him, he's moving here and going to be an hour away from his parents and friends. For him that is what makes it 10 times harder. I am very lucky that I get to live in the same town as my sister.

I don't think he has been in another placement before this, of course I don't know this and I didn't feel like it was my place to ask straight away. Just like I don't feel its right to ask why these kids got put into care. Of course, I want to know and I am interested, but like I said it is still not my place to know, I am interested not because of who they are, but because I really like hearing other people's story. It makes me feel like I am not so different after all. If they wanna tell me then that is up to them.

Brandon is a really cool guy and I think he will like it here; he is going to be moving into Mikes old room as that was the only room with no one in at the moment. With Brandon that made us a 'family of 5 kids'

Sweet Sixteen

Finally, it is here, my birthday and in the eyes of social, finally classed as an adult. I have been waiting to turn 16 for what feels like for ever. I finally have a say in what I do in my life and I am able to make my own decisions for what I want my life to turn out like.

I woke up supper early, ever since I was younger I always use to wake up at 6:40 because that is what time I was born, it was like a ritual. Although I haven't woken up this early in forever.

For once I didn't actually have to set an alarm though, I just woke up at like 6:30 and walked down stairs and had a fag. I gave night staff a little bit of a shock, they weren't use to me seeing me up this early, unless I didn't go to sleep the night before. Also 6;45 is when hand over usually starts so it was nice to see staff arriving on shift as well. The night staff decorated down stairs, with banners and balloons and it was just so so sweet. Literally felt speechless walking down stairs.

If I am being honest, I can't remember who exactly was on shit because not everyone stood out to me on that day. Only really the people, who made some effort for my birthday. They don't have to and they don't get paid to, but some of them choose to.

Clair walked in with this Dr pepper tower, with a big 16 on top and little swirl ribbon dangling down over the Dr pepper. She did inform me that she might get into a little bit of trouble if all of them were full, so she hid 2 full ones in their (on the bottom).

I really wanted to drink one however, I didn't wanna ruin it just yet, so I thought I would wait until a little bit later on in the day.

It was a week day, so all the other kids were getting up ready to go to school and I was sitting at the table opening my cards. I had loads this year! I got a few from staff at Woodmans, a card that every staff member signed from redwood and also probably the sweetest thing I got from the home was a letter from the newest boy- Brandon.

He wrote me a letter saying happy birthday, he had only been here a week and he felt really bad he didn't get me anything, which he didn't have to get me anything, he wasn't to know and he didn't exactly get planned to move here. In the letter is also said "you are a beautiful, powerful independent young lady who can do anything she wants if she puts her mind to it". Honestly Brandon is the sweetest young man I have ever met, especially only considering he's 14.

Even though it was my birthday I still had to go to my lessons, I only had maths to day which I was glad about (I actually like my maths tutor). When I was younger, I always use to ask mum for a sick day because if you go to school on your birthday then that's basically your day over. I think the lesson was only gonna be for 2 hours and it started at 12, so still had ages left until I had to be there.

After that mum was gonna pick me up from the mix and come down Redwood, with Kacey. It was all agreed because usually visitors aren't allowed in before school time. I was shocked Kacey was allowed in as she was supposed to be banned from something that was completely blown out of proportion, but that is just a different story for another time.

Then in the evening it was planned for Kacey and Zak to come round and kinda have like a birthday party, which is also weird because Zak is banned for exactly the same reason as Kacey. At least they could be somewhat understanding on my birthday, they are not complete monsters.

I honestly cannot wait until later, like I have never been so excited for one day in my life. I am a little sentimental because I love birthdays, not such a huge fan of Christmas, but birthdays are like my thing. Even other people's birthdays because that is the one day all about them and you have a chance to make that one person feels so special, even if it is just for one day.

In the morning I was slightly bored though, I still wasn't allowed wifi and they tried to persuade me to do some school work here, I voted against it. I thought I might as well just start getting ready for the day and maybe tidy my room. As I have time why not?

So, I had a shower, straightened my hair, my hair does not hold a curl very well, even though I prefer it curly. Did my every day make up, nothing extravagant, by the time I had pissed about upstairs it was basically time to go.

I still had to walk to the mix though, they said they weren't gonna take the car for a 5-minute trip up the road. Which is fair enough I was just being a little lazy. I thought I would ask because if you don't ask you don't get.

So, as I said it was just maths today, so it wasn't that bad and she brought me a birthday cake as well. Which was a double chocolate cake, it was very yummy, but very sickly. So, me and my tutor each had a piece and then I took the rest back with me. She suggested that it might be nice with some cream, so I was planning to try that later.

With my exams right around the corner the tutors are basically there to help me with what I have revised on. So I revise the days I don't have the tutors and then when I have the tutor's that is my opptunity to ask any questions I might have and if I am stuck on anything, or anything I am unsure with. Although I still have to do some work with her and she does have set topics that she knows usually get brought up in exams, so that's what we usually focus on first, but because it is my birthday, she did let me finish early and she didn't make me do that much work and we eat cake. It was a pretty decent lesson.

After I was done I went straight to the YMCA as I was literally here and as I finished early mum wasn't hear yet, but because I was 16 like I could actually hang out in Kacey's room without staff telling me off.

For any one that doesn't know the Ym is kinda like next to/ under the mix. At the mix's front entrance, theirs like a hill with a massive gate. Through those gates you get to the mixs garden/ Ym's garden. Then you come to the Ym's front door basically.

Mum came about 30 minutes later, she said she ran late at work and there was traffic on the way here. We just got straight in the car and headed to Redwood, theirs this road opposite the mix and that's where we met mum. As there are gates to the mix and it's easier to meet across the road instead of her coming down there. Mums driving at best is average, so didn't want her to do unnecessary turning around.

At redwood we just chilled opened presents, had some more cake. It was nice for mum to be here, she met some of the staff. It was good for her to meet them and for her to get to know who's caring for me. As I moved in here at 15 she don't really need talk much to staff, redwood trust me and so does mum.

Also, it's a little different as I'm on a full care order, mum doesn't have parental responsibilities over me anymore. The local authority does, so although mum has a right to no things I get up to, Redwood isn't legal obliged to tell her. Also, it means that mum can't make big decisions about me. For an example, if I needed an operation, staff at Redwood or social services would make that call.

When the other kids started getting in from college and school that's when mum thought about leaving. She knew I wanted to spend the evening with my friends and family and she didn't want to impose any more. I tried to tell her that she wasn't imposing, but she wouldn't listen and she doesn't like driving back in the dark. Even though it wasn't that dark. My mum is like the queen of excuses.

Zak didn't live at Ym any more so I sent him a message when he was allowed to come down. When he got down here, we listened to some music and played pin the tail on the donkey. It was really dorky, but really fun. It was like the 10-year-old party I never got to have.

As always though Zak had to somehow make it about him. He was telling all the stories about when he used to live here. Even though me and Kacey didn't care, but that didn't stop him anyway. Me and Kacey was making comments which was making everyone else laugh apart from Zak, I don't think Zak got the jokes.

This night was also the first night that me and Beatrice had a bit of a falling out. I was pissed that she had hardly saw me today, like I get I don't own her and I wasn't trying to, but she was my favourite person who worked here. I just thought she would wanna spend some time with me, instead of Robert. After all it is my birthday.

I squared up to her and when I did, she did something pretty amazing, she didn't get mad or angry. She didn't threaten to make my friends leave. All she did was bop me on the nose and said chill out. It just made me laugh and it forget about being angry. Their needs to be more people like Beatrice.

When Beatrice first arrived on to the shift today, she did surprise me with a little present, which I wasn't expecting at all. Technically speaking it wasn't allowed, but Me and Beatrice had a very special relationship. It's almost like she was my mother in a past life or something because at this point, we had only known each other for not even a month and I have never connected to someone this quickly, ever.

I got to pick my birthday meal and I wanted a fry up for dinner. My favourite food is bacon I could eat it all day every day. It was family style, everything had their own dish and we got to serve our self's, favourite type of meals. One thing I do like about redwood is that we always sit at the table, just made it feel more homely.

Not only was today my birthday, but it was also pancake day. So, before Zak and Kacey had to go, we were just in the kitchen flipping pancakes and making them. Zak of course wanted to be the best, but he just wasn't.

After this we also cut the cake. My cake was amazing it was a princess cake with a tiara and sparklers and it was exactly what I wanted. 2 layers that were red velvet.

Me, Nanny and Zak walked Kacey home, as I didn't feel comfortable about her walking home by herself.

Today has been an amazing birthday, it couldn't have been better if I tried. I saw my mum my sister and my boyfriend. It was just perfect!

Moving to the flat

I don't know whether I have mentioned, but at redwood there is a flat, still connected onto the house, but it is just basically a flat. You can only go in their once you turn 16 as it is classed as supported accommodation. Although you are only allowed to be in their if you are on good behaviour and really do want to be half independent. You get to work on your passport to independence, that's what they call it.

Mackenzie already lived in the flat and Robert moved in their shortly after I moved into Redwood. Although Roberts behaviour wasn't acceptable to live in the flat. He was swearing at staff, kept his room a shit hole, but I think the bottom reason was because he was caught smoking in the flat. That's when they said enough is enough!

A shame for Robert, but that meant I have the opptunity to move in their when I was 16. I made sure I was doing what I needed to be doing because it's what I wanted and when I want something I usually am able to get it.

I let Susan aware that's what I wanted and she said to me "I don't think that's going to happen because Mackenzie is already in their". At first, I was confused as to what she meant, but then I asked her "is it because I am a girl?"

She hesitated before she responded to me and she said "well theirs already a boy in there, so it wouldn't be appropriate."

I get it I do, but at the same time why shouldn't be allowed to be in the flat just because Mackenzie is in there. I wanna move in their because I want to grow and learn new skills, skills that I probably could learn in this side of the house, but they wouldn't be semi-independent. So why should I have to jeopardise my future because I am a female because that is basically what they are saying, Robert got to move in there, so I should be allowed.

I get there are worries, I get that and it's no secret that I like guys, but Robert is also bi sexual. Mackenzie is a guy, so something might have happened between Mackenzie and Robert.

See the thing is, is they didn't care about that, all they care about is covering their arse and looking at me and noticing that I am a female, the only female in the house I might add. Also, can I just add my current bedroom is not even 5ft away from another boy's bedroom. So, what is the difference of me being in here than in the flat. If they thought I was going to have sex with another kid here then why place me here in the first place. If that is the only card, they have to play to keep me out of the flat then they are going down. Just because I was born with a vagina doesn't make me easy, doesn't make me a slut and doesn't make me want to have sex with kids in here.

I seriously think this is unfair and I am not going to get told that because I am a female, I can't have something I want. Susan clearly wasn't having any of it so I started to talk to different members of staff and I talked to Susan's boss- Jenny Dean.

Jenny dean manages all the kids homes and basically keeps the managers in check. So, the first person I talked to was Christopher because he was my head key worker and also, he had been here for a good few years, I think at least 6. I asked him if it was going to be possible at all. He said "a boy and a girl has shared the flat before".

So now I know it has happened before, so if I go to Jenny, she will most likely get Susan to change her answer about me moving in there. I know Susan wasn't going to listen to me, but she had to listen to Jenny.

I get Susan is kinda knew, but she needs to learn that you can't make sexism comments and single me out. I ain't that kinda girl any more, I am not gonna bow down and watch things happened around me when I can change them.

You guys might be thinking this is only over a flat and they have serious worries about it. I would class myself as a feminist, but feminism might not mean what you think it means. I believe in equality, men and women should have an equal chance at the same thing and the only thing that should affect it is if they meet the criteria necessary.

Women have come a long way in a 100 years and they only came a long way because women finally had enough of being treated a certain way. So yes, it is just a flat, but I genuinely feel like Susan is keeping me from being in the flat because I am a female.

What also believes me to believe this, is because she makes snarky comments about being a female. Like 'that's not lady like', 'come on immie have some respect for yourself'. These comments were made when I was burping or farting or when I was flirting with Zak or because I was wearing booty shorts around the house.

The boys in this house fart and burp more than I do, I am flirting with my boyfriend I have been in a relationship with and Mackenzie walks around without a top on most of the time. She sees all of this and doesn't say anything to them about it. Rant over! I took it further enough was enough.

A couple of days after my 16 birthday I got told that I had been amazing with my education, been sticking to my curfew and have just been amazing. So, on the weekend if I want to move into the flat I can. I was over the moon! Susan didn't tell me, Christopher did, still Susan didn't look to happy about it, but I didn't care. I got what I wanted just like I said I was going to.

Once you have been in care long enough or around the system, you start noticing what you need to do to get what you want. Sometimes screaming and shouting makes you feel better, but they ain't gonna listen. The biggest weapon you can have is your voice, just remember you are in charge of what happens to you, only you can decide your future and don't ever let your voice not be herd.

Moving into the flat was so long though. It was like moving all over again, without boxes. I made a lot of trips and had to decide where to put things all over again. The flat room was at the front of the flat. When you go in the flat straight ahead of you, you have the kitchen and living room, which has sofas, everything you need to cook and a tv. To the right you have my room and then straight down the corridor you have the bathroom, which doesn't have a bath, just a shower. Then next to it you have Mackenzie's room. Mackenzie actually switched rooms after Robert moved about because that room is slightly bigger, but I wasn't fussed if I am being honest.

The room was so much smaller than the room I was in, but I was okay with that, just meant I have to keep it tidy more. I was just really excited to start my next level of independence and finally start my journey into adult life.

Although I wanted to start my adult life, I still am only 16 and in the eyes of the law I am not an adult yet, but in the eyes of social I was an adult. Something seems very wrong with that. Just because you have a birthday doesn't mean you are ready for some of the responsibilities that come with it.

There was this one time where I was struggling to put the duvet cover on my duvet. I'm 5ft 4, I am small and I struggle to do it. Especially as it's a double bed. I went down stairs and asked Beatrice for help, so she could show me one last time.

Daphne was talking to Beatrice when I asked her and she just said "why".

Nothing was more belittling than that, why? Was a stupid question to ask. I don't understand why should she just say why like that. Why the fuck do you think, genius. You fucking idiot.

For the first few weeks the lounge/ kitchen was locked off in the flat. They were a privilege to have and even though I have earned to be in the flat they would only be unlocked when staff knew I wasn't going to abuse it.

My first job

I have always wanted a job ever since I was like 14, I enjoy having money and I like being able to spend my money. One night I decided to do something about it, I applied for all the jobs I could find, jobs that were most likely going to hire me.

I started applying just after exams had finished. I didn't know if it was going to be a summer job or if I was going to bail on college all together. I have never been academic smart or really street smart. I prefer doing practical things, like dancing or sports. I didn't know if college would be the right fit for me any way. For right now I just wanna keep my options open.

I didn't think I did well in my exams, I was only taking the core subjects, maths, English and Science. On my mocks I didn't do too good, my head was all messed up and I was still at Kez grave when I took them which is why I think I didn't do too good.

I was taking the lower set of exams. There is a lower and a higher set of exams. On the lower set the highest you can get is a C, on the highest, the highest you can get is an A* and the lowest you can get is a C. the teachers and social thought it would be best if I stick to the lower set, they thought I would be able to do the higher, but they didn't wanna risk me coming out with an ungraded. I agreed, my aim was to get at least 1 C and then I would be happy. I had missed the whole of year 10, actually I would be happy just to get some GCSEs from my high school experience.

I got a call about 2 weeks later for a waitressing job at Rushbrooke arms. I had an interview in a week. I was excited, but I didn't know what to wear or how to act. I mean we did learn a few things about it in PSHE, but sometimes what they teach isn't exactly what goes on in the real world.

I talked to redwood about it if they could give me a ride to and from the interview. I just hope they say yes and that they are supportive about this job. I want money to do things with my life, save up for driving lessons, a house maybe or even just to get drunk on the weekend. You just need money in life and as you get older the more money you want. Money doesn't buy you happiness, but it's a good place to start.

All they said is they would have to see what was going on that day. I don't even know what that means, like I need to know. I can't just see if they are able to on the day, what kinda impression does that leave if I can't get there. It makes a difference going by car or by train. They are actually ridiculous!

This was until Tilly actually said that she's in on that day and she can take me in her car. She was honestly a life saver; this could be a big opptunity for me. I get it is only a waitressing job and it's probably going to pay shit, but at least I will have a job and I can start paying my way in the world. These days it is so difficult to find a job and actually get a career and the truth is now I'm not sure what I wanna do when I grow up.

I did wanna be a social worker, but I don't agree with their morals and doesn't look like I am going to be going to uni after all. Always dreamt of going to University of East Anglia and studying social work there. Their campus is lovely, I went on a trip there and stayed there one time in the summer. It was so gorgeous. Although because I am a heavy sleeper, they had to get the spare key because they thought I did a runner or I was dead. Likely I wasn't sleeping naked!

What also was decent of Tilly is she helped me prepare for my interview. She works in recruitment, so she basically deals with this stuff on a daily. She lent me a shirt and suggested of good things to say. Also said smell is really important so spray perfume before, but not too much.

The day of the interview… it was an earlyish interview, about 10ish. I was so nervous I just hoped I wouldn't say something stupid or do something stupid. I just hope they like who I was enough to hire me. At the end of the day, I am not going to pretend to be someone else, I come as I am and if they don't like it then I don't want to work there any ways because I am who I am.

The drive their Tilly helped me with my nerves and said I had nothing to worry about and even if I didn't get the job at least I will have some interview experience and I can learn for next time.

I went through the bar entrance of the pub/restaurant. I said to the bar man "I'm here for an interview". He showed me where to go, I had to fill out this form, it was basically my experience and what my availability would be like if I was to get the job.

There were a few other people here also for the interview, which just made me more and more nervous. They were all older than me from what they looked like, which means they probably had way more experience than me.

I was interviewed by both of the assistant managers. I think it went amazing, so much so they offered me a trial shift then and there. I was so excited, it was slightly hard to keep the excitement in, but I wanted to act like a grown up not a little girl, but when they offered me the trial shift I was just beaming.

The day of the trial shift- Redwood agreed to take me to the trial shift and actually this time I was taken by Beatrice. I thought it would only be an hour because I have never had one before. So, Beatrice said she will be back in an hour.

When I walked into the pub I met with Lacy and she said that Laura will be giving me the trial shift today. Lacy is one assistant manager and Laura is a supervisor. Laura gave me a little tour of out back and told me what sections where what and how the till worked. They weren't gonna expect me to know everything on this first day, but as long as I showed initiative, then I should be okay. They wanted to see me wanting to work here.

I think I was getting the hang of it and I think Laura loved it as I was basically doing her work for a little bit. It lasted longer than I thought, I think it lasted about 2 hours and then at the end of it when Beatrice came in, we all had a sit-down meeting. She offered me the position then and there. I was so happy and I couldn't wait to tell everyone when I got back.

I just had to sign a few things of, mainly to do with health and safety and once they had a contract written then I would sign that when I first start. I was just so happy and I couldn't believe I have actually got a job. It pays weekly as well, so as well having pocket money and incentive money I will have my actually wages. I am very happy.

I know earlier I talked about having pocket money and incentive money from the kids home, well now I am in the flat I get flat chore money. These are done every week, if they aren't done then the money doesn't get rolled over to the next week, like pocket money does. With flat chores you can earn up to £7.50 each, but most of the time Mackenzie didn't do his, so I got an extra £7.50. So, in total I could earn up to £15 a week just in flat chores.

The day I got my ped.

After I got my job, I was so eustatic and I couldn't believe it, but the home was not supportive of it at all. They didn't care about it; they didn't support me in any way other than throughout the interview process. I don't get why they are supportive around education and college, but when it comes to work, they literally just forget about it and it comes last.

This job is so important to me, so sometimes I would catch a train and then a taxi. Or I would ask the home to take me to mums and then mum would take me to work. Which is just so stupid. I know the home cannot refuse to take me to family contact, but my mum lives in Sudbury. You literally go past the pub I work at on the way down there and if they can take me to family contact surely it would just be easier to take me to work.

The lack of support is ridiculous. This job should be something they should be proud of, they should be proud of me and I don't understand why they're not. The only person who was, was Beatrice.

I couldn't keep affording to get a train and a Taxi up there, I was only on £5 an hour. Which was still good for my age, but still not amazing. Although the tips there was really good. In one shift I made about £60 once and that was only for about 5 hours. Even though the tips are amazing, they aren't garneted.

I spoke to this guy who has helped me out in the past and we spoke about this scheme called wheels to work. They basically supply you with a mode of transport, me being 16 I can only get a ped and all it cost is £35 a week. You also have to give a £75 deposit just in case anything happens. I still thought it was pretty amazing, especially when the train up there was a £5 even with my rail card and a taxi was £7.

The great thing is, is that even though you have the ped for work, you still can use it whenever you want. They supply all the gear you need to be safe on the road, they pay for the CBT. It's a scheme that encourages young people to start working and takes the struggle such as transport out of the occasion.

When I had my CBT I was so nervous and scared, the last time I rode a ped was at Woodmans, it was Ryan's and I nearly crashed it into the fence or the car. I didn't ride it properly, but I think it's a good job I didn't actually try and ride it properly because I would hate to see the outcome.

It wasn't so bad, I actually enjoyed it when we finally were allowed onto the road. There are 2 parts to the CBT. The first part; we were at the old sugar beet factory in Ipswich. To learn how to stop and had to do this figure of 8 which was very difficult. I nearly ran over my tutor.

Then we stopped and had lunch. For the second part we went out on the road. When we were on the road, we had an ear piece so we could hear what the instructor was saying but he couldn't hear us. He was able to give us instructions to make sure we were able to basically drive on the road. I was doing my CBT with someone called Charlie, he was learning to drive a 125 instead of a ped.

The great part about this scheme is that they gave me all the equipment to keep me safe, it cost about £250. They gave me a helmet, jacket, high vis. I was meant to get some gloves, but they never gave me it. I could keep these after as well, which is very nice of them to do that.

When I went to go pick up my ped, Christopher took me in the care home car to Ipswich and I rode my ped back. Even though peds are allowed on A roads, we chose not to go along the A14. Especially as this ped wasn't de restricted and it's so dangerous to go slow on a road that's going 70mph. I could easily slide under neath a lorry. I also wouldn't say I'm the most confident driver either, so I just didn't want to and Christopher wouldn't put me in that much danger. We went the back roads home, he had to keep pulling over as cars kept over taking me.

I'm not good with instructions and I have never driven on the back roads home, so I wasn't even able to say to Christopher go ahead and I will just see you at home because I don't think I would be able to find the way back. This did mean that this journey took longer than what it did in the car, but this ped gave me a sense of independence.

It was an enjoyable journey back, I got use to the ped with someone else their instead of figuring things out by myself. Even though I was alone, I wasn't really alone as I could see him checking on me in his mirror regularly. I bet he was slightly scared. For Christopher it must have just felt like a proud dad moment.

I just finally felt like everything was going my way for a change and my life was actually getting on track. I was so excited for my 'grown up' life to finally begin. Finished my exams, got a job and now I have a ped. Just gotta work towards a car and a flat and then I am sorted for a while.

I have a story about my ped which I think is very funny. A staff member from Bury kids home came to do a shift here and he parked next to the home's car. Well, I thought it would be really funny to put my ped in between his car and the homes car.

When he had finished his shift, he came out and was just like oh my god. He asked me to move my ped, I had been drinking, so I just said "I can't I am under the influence." Which was true.

No one knew what to do they were just thinking what could be done about it. If I am being honest, I am not sure exactly what the outcome of it was, but I just look back at it being one of the funniest moments there. It doesn't sound that funny, but trust me is was.

A new kid coming

So it is that time again, a new kid was coming to visit. You guys probably know how it goes down by now, but if this kid moves in then it's going to be a full house. This is the first time that it was going to be a full house, I think, since I have been here.

I knew more about this kid, he was currently living with my old foster carers, Martha and Roy. They wanted to foster him full time because he originally went there as an emergency placement. They knew it took him a while to settle in there, mostly because of his past or something. They wanted to create a home for him, somewhere, where it is somewhat normal. Martha and Roy have this massive house, has sky tv, has dogs, has other kids their as well and a massive garden. I think simple things as dogs makes a house more like aa home and they actually are good for anxiety.

Martha didn't tell me his back story, but she knew that I lived there and all she did say was look out for him. She just said that he is very anxious and doesn't cope with new situations very well. You could see when she was talking about him, she did genuinely care about him. It is such a shame that social won't let him stay with these guys.

His name is Tyson and he's 11. He's honestly so cute, but shy. When he got to the house, I tried making him more at home. We have a PlayStation at the home and I suggested he could go on their and just chill until dinner was done, staff said it was okay. I think anything to try and put him at ease and know that this house can be fun.

Having an 11-year-old in the house is going to be so weird. Like that is a big age gap and I know things are about to change around here. It's going to be different having a younger kid in the house. Yes, there are only 5 years between us, but a lot happens from when your 11-16. Although there is quite a lot of age difference there is such a variety in ages at the moment. We have two 17-year-olds, one 16-year-old, one 14-year-old, one 13-year-old and now an 11-year-old.

As he had some where he could stay, he was going to be having a sleepover kinda thing so he could see how the home is run at night time as well. He was going to be moving into my old room as that's the only room that was available. I personally think it's the biggest room in the main side of the house.

I think everything went so well. It just scares me, change is a very scary thing even when you have changed things almost as much as you change your clothes, but it never gets easier. There are slight changes that don't really affect you like changing your shampoo, but there are massive changes that can affect the whole outcome of your life. It is scary to think that anything could change the impact of your life big or small and you won't know it has changed, until it is too late. This is some proper deep thinking!

It came the day that he was moving in, I went with him to get his stuff. It was good to see Martha and Roy again and all their dogs. Only one dog was still there, from when I was living there- Littlern, he's a Jack Russel cross something, I think. They also have 3 German Shepard's who are just so lovely and cuddly. It was really sad that some of his stuff was in bin bags and also it was surprising to see because that got banned a couple of months ago, I think. I believe that foster carers or social workers had to supply the child with a suitcase if they didn't already have one. I want to know why Martha, Roy or the social worker thought this would be, okay? Social workers I get, they don't care as much, but didn't expect this from Martha and Roy.

His first night in the home was definitely an eventful one at that. It was a decent day outside so in the evening we all went out in the garden and had a little kick about. It was quite nice, but something happened. For whatever reason Tyson called me a tramp, I dunno why? It appeared to be out of nowhere and it pissed me off. I said to him, "do you know what that means?" He didn't say anything. Then I started to raise my voice and shouted at him saying "don't call me a fucking tramp unless you know what it means." He started crying.

I felt awful, who the fuck shouts at an 11-year-old, I was supposed to be the kind one, I was supposed to look out for him and his first night here I shouted at him. The reason it pissed me off so much is because when I lived my mum, I was a tramp. My mum's house was dirty and I didn't have clean clothes and I didn't have a bath in weeks.

That wasn't my fault, that was my mum's fault because it was her duty to care for me and it was her responsibility to make sure I learned how to do these things and it was her responsibility to make sure I was clean. I got called a tramp a lot and that's because I was. So, when someone calls me something I know I am not, I am going to take offense to it and I have a right to be pissed off about it. Sure, I could have handled it in a completely different manor, but I haven't learnt to control my anger yet.

I have come a long way from living at home and I have learned a lot. Just simple things like how to wash my hair properly. I take pride in the way I look and I think first impressions matter. So my big thing is if I meet you, the first 2 things I notice is your teeth and your smell. They tell you a lot about how you live and how much you take in your appearance. You shouldn't matter what people think about you, but you should take pride in personal hygiene and you should care what you think of yourself.

We soon made up. I apologised and said I was completely out of order. I was older than him I should be setting an example. So I also said, "even though I'm sorry how I went about it, what you said was not okay and you shouldn't use words that you don't understand and that aren't even true." He apologised for what he said as well. In this house it is very hard to hold grudges. We are family after all.

Holiday 2017

This is my first time having a holiday in a kid's home. I didn't get one at Woodmans because of the whole closure thing. I was really excited, it was only going to be for a week and it's not like it was abroad, but still I was so excited.

So how it was going to work was, Redwood hired 2 caravans at Hopton in Great Yarmouth, they needed 4 members of staff to go with us, so there could be 2 for each caravan. Not all the kids were going. Mackenzie stayed at home and also Brandon stayed at home. So only 4 kids ended up going, so it was like one member of staff for each kid.

The members of staff going were…Tinisha, Christopher, Victoria and Damian. Damian, is a part time member of staff and he usually always comes on the home's trips. Victoria, just wants all the extra money she can get, she's jetting off to Australia soon. She says she's coming back and I'm the only one that no's that's bullshit. Even Victoria thinks she's going to be coming back.

Me and Robert were going to be sharing one caravan with Tinisha and Victoria. Then Christopher and Damian were going to be having Tyson and Brody in the other one. As I was the only girl, I had to have at least one female member of staff in with me. I ain't sharing a caravan with all boys, that is just not happening.

I was sceptical about sharing with Robert though because he is so messy and disgusting. I love him like as brother, just some days he gets on my nerves. He has to have the attention from staff like all the time and his energy is just so draining.

I was gutted Mackenzie wasn't going to be coming, he was staying at his girlfriends for the week we were away. Yes, I am that girl. Me and Mackenzie have had a thing going on since I was 14, but something has always gotten in the way of us actually being together. We have been talking for a while now, like talking talking. I am a horrible person because I know he has a girlfriend and I still entertain it, but he shouldn't be doing it in the first place.

Doesn't make what I do wright at all, but I can't help it if I like him. We were getting close and I didn't know what to do.

Mackenzie was saying he loved me and saying that he wanted to be with me, but he couldn't break up with his girlfriend just yet as he feels bad for her. Mackenzie is just too sweet for his own good, she doesn't sound like a nice person and she doesn't sound like she deserves him. Writing this I just know I sound like a horrible person.

Although I wanna be with Mackenzie, I just don't think we would work out. Our relationship is very physical. Like he's so gorgeous and really really attractive and I would happily fuck him, but other than that we don't talk about much.

On the trip over there, we had to take 2 separate cars because there was a lot of us. It was such a road trip vibe on the way over. Me and Robert were in one car and we are just bad influences on each other. We play loud music, sing our hearts out and just have an amazing time. Me and Robert just egg each other on all the time.

I just couldn't wait for this holiday; I had already had one about a month ago with Kacey and Jacob. We went to Clacton on sea! I had such a blast; it was my first 'grown up' holiday. Kacey was over 18, she was allowed to be in charge of me, its scary to think that Kacey was actually my guardian over that week.

We went swimming, went to the beach, arcades and of course did loads of dancing in the evening. There was this guy who worked there, he literally looked exactly like Sheldon off the big bang theory. It was so creepy! But all the staff there was really nice. Usually when you go to holiday parks, it is super all about kids, but this one wasn't. There were a few kid's things in the evening, but it kinda all stopped by like 7.

Me and Kacey also had a crush on this guy their, who was just like a proper cheeky person. He must have been at least 28, but still very nice to look at. We can look, but we can't touch, right?

This one is going to be my second holiday of the year and this summer I am such in a holiday mood. For once it has been a hot English summer and I cannot wait to get a tan, well, hopefully. Usually I love winter, I still love winter a lot, but it's nice when you can actually go out and do things again, like just sit in a park and have a picnic.

When we got there, we had to collect our keys and figure out where the hell we were. This is something I am not good at, so I just stood outside and had a fag. There was like a mascot thing. Not sure what they are called? But usually when you go to holiday parks there are these characters.

When I was little, we always use to go to Pontins in Lowestoft on holiday and the characters there were a monkey, zebra and well you get the picture. This one was a life guard. Me and Robert took a photo with it because why the fuck not. Yes, people were starring, but we are here to have fun so that is exactly what I am going to do and nobody is gonna stop that.

As soon as we got to the caravan, I ran out and got the double bed. No way was I letting Robert have a double bed for 5 days. That room comes with an ensuite so it was mine. Tinisha and Victoria was adamant that they wanted that room just because it was bigger, but I wasn't giving it up for anybody. This is my holiday and I am going to spend it how I want to. If Mackenzie was here, I would share this room with him, but I am not sharing with anyone else. Jokes…kinda!

I get it, it's is their holiday as well, but they wouldn't be getting a free holiday if it wasn't for us. Primarily this is the kid's holiday, sure staff should have a good time, but at the same time they still need to act as our carers.

Our holiday was self-catering, so we still had to cook our own food and Christopher had accounted for that. We were also given a budget of how much money we had for an activity each day. If we didn't spend money on activity for a day we had more money to spend the next day, I think that makes sense. Although I had wages from work so I didn't really care. I brought £200 with me because I wanted to buy Kacey a present.

Because of course some days we would just wanna spend by the beach or in the pool and because they all came with the caravan; we didn't have to pay for any of that. The one thing I hate when I go on holiday is a schedule.

I get it's nice to have some sort of an idea of what you want to do, but at the same time enjoy it and take each day as it comes. As it is a kid's home holiday, I doubt it is going to be like that because they have to cater for everyone's needs and some people like to have

structure and like to know what they are doing.

The plan was for now, to unpack, get settled in and then we were going to go down to the

arcades and to the club house part. Like I said we have to cater for everyone. Yes, I like going down to their, but at the same time I don't like watching the kid's stuff. I am not even

allowed to stay in the caravan by myself, so I had to go with them.

We had drinks, non-alcoholic of course. Then we danced and had a laugh, every one Was having a good time. It was just a really good night and if this is, is the start of the holiday I can't wait for the rest of it.

The next day I woke up really early actually, I had such a nice sleep and was so excited for the day to start. I dunno why I woke up so early, I mean I definitely didn't do this when I had to go to school. Just today felt like a good day and I was ready for it to begin. As I felt amazing, I decided to go for a run, I hadn't been for one in ages and I just find a run really gets you ready for a good day.

I didn't run for long, my legs could have continued, but my lungs couldn't. I have asthma and I smoke. I should definitely stop smoking, but yeah ain't that simple. After my run I had a shower and ate some breakfast, I'm not really a breakfast person, so this is surprising for me. I kinda wanted to go to the beach today, but the weather looks like its gonna rain. So, it might be the swimming pool and then the beach later, it all depends on the weather.

After I had sorted out my hair and make-up everyone was pretty much awake and then we discussed what we might be doing for the day. We had to check what the other kids wanted to do. Like I get it, but I am 15 if I wanna do something for myself, why can't I. Surely, I should be allowed, but I weren't gonna have an argument I want to continue to have a nice day. So, for once I left it!

Whilst the other kids were getting ready, it actually got really sunny, we didn't know how long it was gonna last for, I mean, this is England. The weather changes all the time. I got my bikini on and like an oversized top and then off we went.

Before we went, whilst I was still getting ready and sorting out my bag out, I asked permission if I was allowed to wear my bikini because we live in a fucked-up world. I mean, at Redwood I wasn't even allowed to wear shorts in the house around the other boys. I think it was right to ask, but the fact is, I shouldn't have to because I'm not in control of what boys choose to think. I should be allowed to wear what I feel comfortable in, here and at Redwood.

Tinisha said "well I am wearing one because I ain't gonna be in a track suit". Honestly Tinisha just cracks me up. She is very honest and very forward with what she says. A little like me I suppose. Sometimes it's a good thing, but most of the time it is a bad thing. The way I look at it is, is I would rather someone be honest with me, instead of lying to my face about it.

The younger boys and the male members of staff were all playing in the sea and the female members of staff, me and Robert were just chilling on the rocks. Taking photos, smoking some fags. I wanted to get a tan, but it ain't that hot here.

I decided I didn't wanna swim in the sea, for one it's going to be freezing, but for 2 swimming in the sea doesn't appeal to me what's so ever.

We spent the majority of the morning down on the beach, we buried Christopher and gave him boobies. It was a really good morning, but we came back to the caravan for lunch. I had plans on what I wanted to do this afternoon, but I know it's gonna be down to the younger kids on what they do. I get its their holiday as well, but its mine to and I wanna be able to enjoy it.

I basically could do what I wanted to do, as when I was at home, I didn't need any supervision to do anything. So here was basically the same as long as I had my phone on and I had their number, it was okay. Although, it was basically a family holiday and why would I wanna do stuff by myself. Because that doesn't sound like fun what's so ever. I'm not gonna be living at the kids home for ever so I should enjoy it while I can.

For the remainder of the days, we went swimming, played on the arcades, went to the beach. In the evening we mostly spent in the little club thing, me and Robert were allowed to spend as long as we wanted there. It was fun, we danced, sang our hearts out and just had an amazing time. What was surprising is we didn't have a set allowance to spend on drinks or anything. Usually Redwood, well just the local authority is very stingy with money.

Although it was a great holiday and I loved it, but there was one incident that fucked me off through and through. 1, because it was just a cunty move 2, because I thought there was more respect between us both and 3, because he knew I wouldn't able to by some more.

What happened was, Robert clearly stole my baccie. I don't have any proof, but I don't need it. At the end of the day, I know how much baccie I had in my pouch. I know where I left it and how I left it and the only other people in the caravan was staff. I am almost positive that they would not steal my baccie because they can afford to buy their own and their old enough to buy their own.

Look if he did it just fucking admit it, own up to what you did and just have the balls to say yeah, I messed up. Like I would still be pissed if he said yeah, I did it. I would be angry and annoyed. But lie to me even though I blatantly know it was you and I am going to be even more pissed off. He knows I can't go and get more baccie because I don't know anyone here and I ain't just gonna go and ask random people.

Honestly, I just don't get why people lie and steal. Like yes, I get why you want things other people might have, but why? Why not just ask? The worse that could happen is I say no.

Then you should respect the decision that I have made. I love Robert like a brother, but omg he pisses me off and the really disappointing thing is he wont change.

Beatrice leaving

The day I dreaded and the day I thought would never happen. Beatrice decided to leave. I came back from mums. I went straight up to my room and Beatrice asked to speak to me and closed the door behind her, something was off with her and that is when I knew.

It's happened to me a lot, when I moved from home to home, when a social worker was leaving or when I kept getting told I wasn't good enough to stay in a place. They always have the same look and expression on their face.

I ran out of the bedroom, ran out of the home and sprinted up the road. I needed to think I needed time to process what the fuck was going on. Beatrice was the mum I never had and the mum I needed. I never thought she would leave me and I didn't think it was going to be whilst I was still living here. I just didn't think it would be this soon.

When I was running up the road, Beatrice was right behind me. She wasn't going to let me think and she wasn't going to allow me time, until she had explained. She wanted to tell me why and she explained that she wasn't leaving me, she was leaving the job. This job wasn't good for her and after she explained I understood and I didn't need time. I just knew when she left, I was going to leave as well.

She said she was leaving because the management wasn't good for her. They just weren't good in general. I didn't know half the stuff that happened because she didn't want me to know because she knew exactly how I could be, but because she was leaving, she told me what the reasons behind her decision.

The management didn't like the relationship me and nanny had, they didn't like how close we were and they thought that our bond with each other was un natural. I think they were very jealous of the relationship we had built with each other, over the short period we had known each other.

Looking back at it now, I can definitely see how management tried to stop Beatrice and me spending time with each other. I just think the whole situation was very unfair. If you have a good bond with a member of staff, why would you try to keep them separate. That just makes no sense to me. Me and Elvis had a good bond with each other, so why didn't they do the same with us?

I think our relationship is funny because I hated her to begin with and I miss judge her so so much and thank god I ended up with her as my key worker. It makes me wonder how much my life would be different if she wasn't my key worker. I know I would never be this close to any other staff there. Beatrice actually took the time to listen to me and understand my issues. Beatrice broke the rules because some times in this job you have to. She was probably the best care worker at Redwood and the ONLY reason she left was
because of management.

Nanny use to do things for me that I will miss, little things, but they made a big impact on my day and mood. Like making my bed for when I got home from work, saving me some dinner. Picking me up from the station after I worked a long shift. It doesn't take much to be kind. She didn't do these things because I asked her to or because I am lazy, she did these things to show how much she cared.

I am still very close to Nanny now, I have been to her house, met her kids and have been accepted as part of their family. Now is the time I wanna say thank you to nanny's husband
and kids for allowing me to be included.

I am a true believer that everything happens for a reason and I truly believe that me and nanny was suppose to meet. She is my mum and I now have older brothers and a new older sister. My family has expanded massively and for that I will be for ever grateful.

Everything changes.

As you guys know, well as I have tried to explain we have had a lot of people moving in and a lot of people moving out and frankly it can get a bit boring, so up until I leave, I thought it would just make sense to tell you about the people that moved in and moved out.

Firstly, there was an 11-year-old called Andy. He was very sweet and very cute. He was so well behaved and I was shocked he was getting put into a kid's home instead of going into foster care. I don't know his story and as I have said I don't want to, that is his story to tell and he should be the one to share it, if that is his decision to do so.

I just didn't like that they are bringing in 11-year-olds because its more likely that the things the elder children want to do, we aren't going to be able to do. Also, since Tyson has moved it has kinda already changed.

Basically, they have just started bringing in new rules. Like staff have to be in the building by 8pm every night. Even though sometimes I don't finish work till like 10. I have to walk home from the station at 10 every night in not a nice area of stow and anything could happen basically, but I don't think they really care about that. All they care about is the younger children living their when really all of the kids at Redwood need support and need to be loved. This is a massive safeguarding issue.

With Tyson they do everything for him when really, they should be teaching him to do these things by himself. Like I am pretty sure he can learn to do his washing and tidy his room. All he needs is staff helping him, or even supporting him.

Obviously with us being a full house in order for Andy to move in some one left. Brody left shortly after holiday, but him leaving was a happy ending. He went to go live with his brother which is what he was working towards any way. I am so happy he got what he wanted in the end.

Secondly there was another boy who moved in after Andy. This boy was called Jason. He was 15 and from Ipswich, but he was like 6ft tall. He did not look like he was 15, he looked more like 17.

When Jason moved in Mackenzie had to move out. He was nearly 18 any ways, so he didn't have a choice. He moved to Bury supported accommodation, which is good because he wasn't far away from his college. Its really where he wanted to go, so I'm happy for him. Slightly pissed that he has gone because we were really close now and not just on a physical level any more.

Hopefully now he doesn't live here we can just continue to grow together and go out and do things and hopefully become a real couple, like both of us have wanted for ages. We did respect the kids home and nothing happened whilst we lived their apart from a cheeky flirt. I mean we didn't even kiss!

With a kid's home, there's always going to be people moving in and out and the staff changing all the time. I literally have no issue with that because that is just life as a care kid, but what I do have an issue with; if it disrupts my life.

I am usually the person disrupting the other kids, but I have managed to turn my life around that I don't really care for being a dick head any more. I have a job, done my GCSE'S, moved into the flat. It's not a lot, but it's a start to a really good life, I have achieved so much more than I could of imagined at 16, I am very grateful for everything I have been blessed with.

I just say this because Jason and Robert just bounce off each other, literally like me and Saph. I know them living in the same house is going to be a bad idea. This is just going to be history repeating its self (kinda).

For example, on a Wednesday night, I think, they were just sitting in Jason's room speaking really loudly, pissing about. Staff were up here as well because they have to be if we are in each other's rooms. My room is in the flat, so to be in my room you have to go through 3 doors and a stair well, but I still could hear it. Which that means they are just being ridiculously loud. Now I am pissed.

I had work at like 11am the next morning, which to be honest isn't really that early when you think about it, but you have to take into consideration I have to eat breakfast and have a shower before I leave and then on top of that I have to catch a train and a taxi. just the little things that mean I have to wake up early, so I can be at work on time.

I just went into Jason's room and literally just had a go at them. The gist of it was "this is so disrespectful, you come into my home and start acting like this, I have to be up in 6 hours." They just sat their laughing once I left. Like what the fuck. I went back in there and just stood there and said "what's funny." I was not gonna leave if they weren't gonna shut the fuck up.

Robert moved out as well, but it was like a month after Jason moved in. So now I was the only person left from the people that were here when I first moved in with and it's kinda sad because it's not like I have been here that long.

However much I dislike Robert, he is still my family and I don't know where I would be without him. I have said this so many times before, but people in my life influence my life in different ways. Also, family is family and I never turn my back on family.

I haven't really spoken much about Jason or his moving in, that's because he does need his own chapter and that is all I have to say on this matter for now, it will be releveled in time. It does get a bit juicy.

Jason, Jason, Jason

As you know Jason moved in, not long after holiday. By then Mackenzie moved out and Robert moved out soon after Mackenzie. There wasn't any of the original bunch left at Redwood. I had been there the longest and I am now the oldest.

Staff expected me to be the role model and set a good example to the younger ones. Which I thought I could do because I had been properly getting my life on track, which I was proud of, as you all can tell. I hadn't felt this in control of my life in a very, long time and it feels great.

I Haven't mentioned Matty at all, I use to live in a foster placement with him, he did live at the YMCA and now he lives just up the road to me in the Benjamin foundation, which is actually where Robert ended moving to.

Any way Me and Matty became really close, he's my best mate and I feel like I can chat to him about anything. He was, is my go-to person. Well, we weren't exactly good influences on each other, weren't bad but we allowed each other to just have a good time and chill.

We were so close at one point that everyone thought we were dating. Matty is like my gay best friend, although he ain't gay.

Well one night me, Matty and Jason were all hanging out. We had been smoking and drinking a little bit. I am not sure who's idea it was but suddenly we were playing spin the bottle. Me and Matty had to kiss, which was just weird for us both because we were mates and that was all. Literally didn't feel right kissing your best mate. Then me and Jason had to kiss, well first it was a kiss and then it turned into a snog.

I weren't mad at it, but it broke my biggest rule, which was don't do anything with people you live with, I know I have done shit with people in the past, but I didn't wanna make past mistakes. This was my fresh start and if you make a mistake for than once it is no longer a mistake it is a choice.

It was a good snog like I can't complain about it, but I thought it would just be a snog and that's it, but later that night he sent me a snapchat. He wanted me to come into his room, so I said "alright." I would never have guessed what happened next.

I was just chilling in his room and then he kissed me again. Things got heated pretty quickly next thing I know he was on top of me and we were fucking. This is technically illegal, I am 16 and he's 15, but trust me wouldn't have guessed he was only 15.

After it was done, he lent on the tv remote whilst trying to get up and the tv went from like 10 to 50. Staff were nearly gonna come up and obviously this is was massively forbidden. If staff found out about this one of us would get moved and it would probably be me because I am the eldest.

We played it off and said I came in here just to get a filter to go down and have a fag, so that's what we did. I was expecting it to be awkward, but it wasn't. I know I wasn't gonna date him or anything because he is immature. I just thought it would be a onetime thing and that was that.

Well from what it looked like it was just going to be that. It happened a week later. And then it happened again. So it was like this causal thing that was just happening and I weren't mad about it.

Although I felt guilty, because me and Mackenzie was getting closer, but he wasn't gonna make it official. I don't know why because we were acting like we were together apart from the label.

Thinking about it now I should of told him I was sleeping with Jason, but if he wasn't ready to make it official I wasn't gonna stop having fun. He wouldn't admit it, but I reckon he was still chatting to other girls because he told me he just got out of a relationship he wasn't ready to jump back in one. Like I get it, but if he's not ready to make that commitment then neither am I.

Mackenzie did do this really sweet thing though! I am 16 and I had never been on a date although I had 3 serious boyfriends, not one of them took me out, but Mackenzie did. We met in Bury and he took me to go play pool.

When we both lived at the kids home together this was our thing. We are super competitive with anything; I remember he was really good at go karting and pool and he kept mentioned he was undefeated. Well, that was until I moved in.

I only won against him once at go karting and quite a few times at pool, but I said "I beat you so that doesn't mean your undefeated." I only needed to beat you once and I did!

Back to the date…we went to bury bowl, which is like a bowling place, but they do have quite a few pool tables there. He brought me a coke and we had chips to share.

He was helping play, even though I don't need it, but you know in like movies and how the guy helps the girl, I think it was like him trying to make a move or something. I think he was being a tad shy. I'm not sure but he was just being the cutest and it was so sweet. I was supposed to have work after, but I didn't want this to end. I called in sick and we went back to his to watch movies, which everyone knows what that means. We started kissing and then one thing led to another and we fucked.

With Mackenzie it wasn't that unexpected, I mean with the messages we had been sending it was bound to happen at some point. I am surprised me and Mackenzie didn't fuck at Redwood to be honest.

Me and Jason were causal up until I left Redwood. We had an understand and we actually became very close, I never thought we would be close. People surprise you when they feel comfortable to trust you.

Another Robert.

As you know Kacey is dating someone called Jacob, well after Christmas I met his brother, Robert. So, we don't get confused with the kid I live with I am going to called Jacob's brother rob.

Me and Kacey went to Ipswich to spend our Christmas vouchers and have a look at all the sales on. Jacob and Rob were coming with us, I had met Rob before, but he had always been with his girlfriend and didn't really talk to me much.

Rob was 24 years old, had blonde hair and was 6ft. Cute in like a dorky kinda way. We just hit is off, we had so much banter between us and it was just amazing. At this point in my life, I had so much going on with Zak that is was just nice to meet someone that didn't have any drama, or didn't care about drama. like Rob is just amazing.

We were just walking around and chatting a load of shit to be honest, I am not a shy person and I am pretty out there. I am also really funny when I wanna be. Rob was just like a breath of fresh air; he was refreshing to be around.

After this day we became texting buddies, kinda? What I mean by that is, ever since that day we didn't stop talking. He always sent me a good morning text and he always made me feel good about myself.

One day Rob randomly messaged me saying "will you be my girlfriend?"

I didn't know what to say, like I knew he liked me and I told him that I liked him, but he asked me this like a day after I broke up with Zak and however much I disliked Zak I couldn't do that to him because I did still love him.

I explained that to him and he got it. He did still wanna continue to talk to me and I wanted to still talk to him, I think he just asked that question to soon. If he said it maybe in 6 months my answer would have been different.

We met up one time, I asked Kacey to come with me because I didn't want to be awkward. I didn't think it would be, but you never know. It was nice to see him, we didn't really do anything just walked around and got to know each other a bit better.

He kissed me; I didn't know what to do. When he did kiss me there wasn't anything there. When I have kissed people before, there has been some chemistry, but this kiss wasn't a good kiss.

He asked me out again and this time I said "I just need a friend not a boyfriend right now". He was slightly annoyed. I think Rob is one of these people that needs a girlfriend to feel complete. Whereas I don't ever need a man if I have a boyfriend, it's because I choose to.

A few months later… I found out that Rob is back with his ex-girlfriend, which turns out they were only on a break. When I asked him why did you get back with her? He just said "because she was there."

He didn't sound like he actually wanted to be in that relationship he just wanted to be in a relationship- if you get what I mean. It's a bit sad really.

Some place better

November 2016, I had an email from a guy called Nathen, he was the head of adoption and fostering in Suffolk, he's not now, but that doesn't matter. He was amazing I had only met him once, but he left a lasting impression.

He wanted to ask my permission to send my book 'care kid' to a theatre company called Red Rose Chain. It's a theatre company in Ipswich, who do a lot for the community and do huge amounts for disabled young adults.

I have Martha and Roy to thank for making this happen. I sent them a draft of my book and they thought people needed to see this, so did I, but I didn't know how to make this happen.

I was overwhelmed that this was happening. Never once did I think this was possible and it was like a dream come true. I met with Jill at Red rose chain who is the artistic director there. We met at Martha and Roy's house, she had already read my draft and was so excited and you could tell she was very passionate about what she does and she loves it. She brought me a present it included, Ted Baker perfume and a pink note book. Which proved she actually did read it and she understood me.

Jill had so many ideas and we set a date to arrange things and to actually put this in motion. In that second, I just felt so excited and I felt like crying with joy. I was 15 and I had already felt like I was making a difference.

When I got back to Redwood, I was so excited to tell everyone about it and what was happening and yeah. There wasn't really much to tell at that moment, but that I was going to have my own play next year. 2017 was going to be my year.

Over the duration of about 9 months, we had regular meetings to discuss what was going to happen and I had a very good input of the whole situation. I was named co-writer, which I basically was, this was my idea and Jill was able to put it in a play format. Jill was very good at the creative side and what would make good for a visual production. My book has a lot of placements and putting them into the style of a play would be a lot.

One of the first things we decided to do was choose which placements we should use and which of the ones had the biggest impact on my life.

We had a meeting a couple of days after my birthday and Jill had brought me flowers, it was literally like she understood me and knew what would make me happy. Whenever I would go there without a doubt, I would always leave smiling and full of life. I knew this is something I wanted to do and things were starting to happen in my life. I just wanted it to happen now and see everyone's faces.

Throughout this year Jill also got me into reading again. I loved reading when I was younger and then I didn't really do it when I went into care because I was doing other shit. Jill wanted to know what books I had read and what I really wanted to read; I have always wanted to read the 'Harry Potter' books. I have seen all the films and in love with them, but I have herd that the books are different to the films and I'm intrigued by that. JK Rowling is an incredible writer and if I can become half the writer, she is then I will be happy.

After I read these books, I couldn't stop reading, I read my child hood book again which was the far away tree by Enid Blyton, then I read the Chocolate box girls by Cathy Cassidy which are amazing.

Red rose chain always has a massive theatre production called theatre in the forest. It's usually based on a Shakespeare play. Whilst the actors are rehearsing for this production, I also got to meet the actors that were going to be in my play. We were only having 2 actors in my play. Jill is very good at creating a whole production not using many actors. I won't lie, I am not really creative, this is what jill does for a living and if she has a vision, I am not going to mess with that. I trust her. The actors are called Jennifer and Amy. Amy was going to be playing me and Jenifer was going to be playing everyone else.

I was also going to be starring in the play. It was going to be this secret; at the start of the show, they would say and now we need a volunteer and every time they would choose me. I was excited, like my acting debut.

One thing that made me laugh though, I told people there was going to be a surprise in it and how exciting it was, etc. When I told Mike this, he thought it was about him. This just goes to show how self-absurd he is.

We still need to discuss things in more detail, but this was purely to see if I wanted to hire them. It was like a very informal job interview I suppose. All they had to do was read a few lines from the draft script. Honestly, they were just amazing and I couldn't imagine anyone else starring in my play.

My play was going to be held at Red Rose Chain from the 18th-21st October and was going to have a one-off performance in London at the N16 theatre. It was all so real and I still am in shock.

On the first of October up until my play we worked really hard. We were at Red Rose Chain from 10am-5pm. And we had weekends off, it was like a proper job and I just really enjoyed being in that environment.

On the first day, it was more deciding what we were going to do and how we were actually going to make the play. Me and Jill both wanted the actors to have an in put because this is a very powerful play and to me it was very important that they understood how I felt at the time these events were happening in my life.

The set was going to made up of card board boxes. The house, the social workers car, even my wardrobe at Woodman's. Jennifer took the lead at figuring out how the boxes were going to be. As it was very important! Some boxes were painted pink and green, some boxes were reconstructed so we were able to sit down on them (used for the social workers car).

I think cardboard boxes signifies a lot with in the care system, your whole life gets thrown in a box, or worse a bin bag. You just get moved from place to place without the foster carers giving a fuck. The 3rd foster placement I went to I was their 5 months and I got kicked out, they didn't sit down with me and have a conversation, I found out by coming back from school with my whole room filled with cardboard boxes as tall as the celling. Jill thought that was a shitty thing to do and people need to see that, this isn't okay.

Jennifer figured out the 'choreography' with the cardboard boxes. Jennifer was playing all the foster carers, social works, my sister and my mum. Literally anyone who wasn't me. Amy was the voice in side my head, what I wanted to say, but what I was too scared to say and I was playing me. What I showed and people saw.

The theme was pink and purple. Everything that me or Amy had to use was pink and anyone that Jenifer was playing was Purple. So, for example I had a pink back pack, pink head phones and a pink jacket.

Kacey was the sweetest and so supportive, she was my rock throughout the whole thing. She came to rehearsal most nights, so she knew everything that was going on and also, she came to basically all my performances. I couldn't off asked for better support because after all she was my number 1 fan.

The first night of my show was the opening night, which of course was the most important. This was the first night that other people got to see my story, so many emotions were running through my head. Jill made it the most amazing experience. There was refreshments and drinks for when people walked in. I was in the dressing room getting ready with the other actors. It just felt amazing.

Thursday was my press night. In all honesty I am not really sure what a press night is because I did a lot of press interviews before hand, to get this play hyped up. Although, when I did these interviews, they didn't see the play. So maybe this was their opptunity to see the play in action so they can write even better reviews about it.

The rest of the shows in Ipswich were a huge success. I had 4 sold out shows and of course the show in London was sold out as well. It really highlighted the care system and their wasn't a bad review about it, or if there was I didn't hear one.

There was such a demand for a longer run and hopefully in the future there will be because I would be happy to do it all over again. The show in London was more a professional kind of vibe, full of directors and actors, people who are in the industry.

When we went to London, I was very sick, I had a sore throat, a runny nose. I was just so poorly, but Jill just got loads of things to make me feel better; paracetamol, Lucozade and this comfy scarf. I just hope I will be alright for the performance tonight because I would be gutted if I missed it. This was the only performance I wasn't going to know anyone in the audience.

This is one of the most memorable experiences I have ever had in my life. I cannot believe I was able to have this and be able to create something like this at just 16. It would not of been possible without the people I have met along the way. So, thank you. You guys know who you are!

My decision to leave

Near the end of my time at Redwood, things weren't going so great. Nanny had left, these younger kids were coming to live here. Things were changing and it wasn't the same Redwood I use to know. I knew that if I didn't make a decision quick, the decision would soon, not be my choice any more.

I had to really think if I wanted to live at Redwood still. There were pros and cons to everything, so I just made a list.

Pros!
- I love living here, love the staff (well most of them), love the kids (most of the time) and this is where I have truly grown as a person. I never thought that I could actually grow up, but Redwood allowed me to and has given me the freedom I needed.
- I have lived here for nearly a year now, but it has been my home for way longer than that. It's not my birth family, but it honestly feels like I have gained a whole new one. The activities, the family dinners, the holidays. Just everything a normal family would be doing.

Cons!
- Younger kids live here now, which mean the rules are changing to cater for their needs and I am the eldest. I am expected to do everything that I don't know if I am ready for. I feel like they don't necessarily have time for me.
- Nanny has left. Nanny was only here for about 9 months, but our bond was just like it was meant to be. Like she had been my mum in a past life or something. I love her so much and well it can never be home without your mum. I call her nanny, but I should call her mum.

- Maybe it is my time to go. Maybe I need to just do it now before I get to out of control again and I have to start from square one. Although now I am 16 it will be so much harder, to grow.

We have more cons than pros. I guess I need to leave and just get it over and done with. My goal any way is to have a flat by the time I am 18 and the best way to do that is to go into supported accommodation.

I want to go into the Ym, where Kacey use to be. I know what it's like, I know some of the staff. I have been going there since I was 14, its pretty much my home all ready.

It is time for me to start my new adventure in life, nothing lasts for ever. Redwood has been fun and I will miss it so much, but like I said the kids I was there with have gone, some of the staff have left and now I think it is my time to do the same.

I contacted my social worker with the decision. She got it, but she doubled checked to make sure this is definitely what I wanted because once it happens there is not turning back.

I had a meeting with Raj, Victoria took me. There were other people in the office. Both of them were staff members. One was very good looking and very nice to talk to, I will not say which one because they might end up reading this and well, that would just be a little bit awkward. Some things are best left un said.

I had a tour around the place, even though I really didn't need one, as I said been coming here since I was 14 I know it pretty well. I was going to be in the exact same room Kacey was in. Room 8. Which was just perfect!

Redwood Lodge I love you, we have had good times and bad times, it wasn't the easiest ride all of the time, but so much easier compared to other places I have stayed. There were laughs, a lot of laughs.

You allowed me to become this stronger, more independent women, you challenged me and that was the best thing you could have done. When I moved to Redwood, I thought I was all grown up and I didn't need help and I wanted to do my own thing. When the truth is, is I only started growing once I let people in.

I didn't like all the staff and that was a secret, but each and everyone one of them made me who I am and for that I will be forever grateful. I want to thank everyone who has been involved in my life in some way. Each and everyone of you has made an impact

Where are they now!

Immie, I am now 20 years old. I actually convinced social to let me have a flat at 17, somehow. I have a gorgeous little boy who is 21 months, who's dad is actually Ryan. I work as a carer for vulnerable adults, but hopes to work at Woodman's next year. She still keeps in contact with Robert, Elvis and Beatrice.

Kacey, Kacey is now 23 years old. She is pregnant with her first child and Immie can't wait to be an auntie. Kacey is no longer in a relationship with Jacob, but has been in another relationship for the past 2 years.

Mackenzie, He has got two kids, with two different women. He doesn't have a job and he lives with his girlfriend's parents.

Robert, he got addicted to coke, but is clean now. Was face book famous for stealing a bike. He has a beautiful little boy and has finally found himself a girlfriend who is willing to put with up with his.

Mike, Mike has been everywhere. London, Norwich, Yarmouth. He met Fleur East so that was pretty cool.

Sapphire, she has been to several mental hospitals looking for the right help for her. She's currently growing weed that she posts on her snapchat story.

Brody, I don't know how he's doing. I assume good.

Brandon, he got too old to live at Redwood and I think he moved back down to Lowestoft. He is still a gentleman.

Tyson, he ended up moving to lowesoft kids home as Redwood couldn't cater for his needs any longer. Also he didn't really fit in with other kids that was moving in to Redwood.

Jason, He's got a flat, got a girlfriend and is expecting his first baby.

Matty, Matty's had a really hard time of it. He struggles, but he knows I am always their if he needs me.

Zak, he's still in prison.

Elvis, he's still working at Woodmans and I sees him quiet often.

Beatrice, she always messages me and makes sure Immies okay. I little boy loves her.

Clair, she left Redwood soon after I did actually.

Christopher, he left to become a detective, but now he's back at Redwood again.

Tinisha, she's still at Redwood, but now she's a senior and well deserved I reckon.

Tilly, shes a senior at bury kids home. I spoke to her quiet frequently once I left and then we lost contact for a little while, but now we are talking again.

Victoria, she never came back to Redwood. So, I don't know what happened to her.

Jill, is still killing it at Red Rose Chain.

Jenny, Retired.

I have probably missed some people, but this concludes the end of my book.

On the 11th March 2021 my grandad died. I didn't always get along with him, but he was the first man I ever respect. I am just sad he's not around to read this book. So, I would like to dedicate this book to him and in his memory. He was very proud of me and my first book. So until we meet again Grandad, keep steering me on the right path.

Printed in Great Britain
by Amazon